Beauty and the Beast
an erotic re-imagining

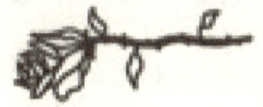

SHOSHANNA EVERS

Beauty and the Beast (an erotic re-imagining)
© 2014 Shoshanna Evers
Cover art by Rob Sturtz SelfPubBookCovers.com

Trade paperback publication, copyright © 2014 Shoshanna Evers

ISBN-10: 0991372220
ISBN-13: 978-0-9913722-2-5

DEDICATION

For my husband, always and forever

.

CONTENTS

ACKNOWLEDGMENTS

Thank you to my readers, first and foremost. Without you, I would be writing into the abyss. *Beauty and the Beast* is written in a different style for me, compared to my other books, and I appreciate that you've joined me for this journey! And a special shoutout goes to the Shoshanna Street Team—thank you for your support, and for spreading the word!

I owe a huge debt to the many incarnations of *Beauty and the Beast* that have come before my erotic re-imagining. While Gabrielle-Suzanne Barbot de Villeneuve and Jeanne-Marie Le Prince de Beaumont are long gone, their stories live on forever.

Thank you to Rob Sturtz of SelfPubBookCovers.com for designing my beautiful cover.

I co-founded SelfPubBookCovers.com with Rob to help fulfill my dream of having quality covers at an affordable price available to all indie authors, instantly. If you're a writer, too, you might want to check out the amazing artists we have on board!

Thank you to bestselling romance author Heather Thurmeier for reading the first draft of *Beauty and the Beast* and providing her insight, and thank you to my wonderful assistant, Annette Stone.

Last on the list but first in my heart: thank you, Dear Husband, for being awesome. I love you!

AUTHOR'S NOTE

The story of Beauty and the Beast has been told and retold in many reincarnations since its debut as a French fairytale by Gabrielle-Suzanne Barbot de Villeneuve, back in the year 1740. The tale we are more familiar with came later, in 1756 by Jeanne-Marie Le Prince de Beaumont. I particularly loved the black and white French movie entitled *La Belle et la Bête*, which was filmed in 1946. And, of course, we cannot forget the Disney musical from 1991.

There have been many, many other adaptations of this classic fairytale, including television shows, songs, operas, ballets and stage plays, and I have researched many of them. But every time I imagined the Beast alone in that castle, with Belle—his beautiful captive—I wondered what could have happened between them that a children's story might omit.

My version of *Beauty and the Beast* is an erotic reimagining. It is *not* a tale for children. I have included some elements from the original fairytales, including how the Beast was seduced by the enchantress, the fairies that seemed to bring their magic to the castle, and the enchanted looking glass. The idea of Belle seeing the Beast's true form in her dreams and searching for him by day in the castle is also inspired by the original tale. You will not find talking clocks or candelabras in my story, nor will you find Belle's brutish suitor, Gaston.

You will find, however, what happens when a young man is imprisoned in the body of a beast—when he can only return to his true self if, and only if, he can find true love, and be loved in return…

...And if that Beast finds his pleasure in the sight of a young woman, bound and at his mercy... and that young woman finds herself entranced by her burgeoning sexuality and the pleasures her experiences with the Beast provide her... well, dear readers—that is my story. The erotic story of Beauty and the Beast.

I hope you enjoy it.

~Shoshanna Evers, December 2013

PROLOGUE

Once upon a time, in a land far, far away, there lived a handsome young prince named Frederick. This is not his story alone, and this is not quite where our story begins. But without what happens here, Beauty would never have met the Beast.

So we shall begin with what occurred on that fateful night when everything changed: when a lover was betrayed, a man deformed, and a castle shrouded in an enchantment.

Frederick smiled as Nadine's dress slipped to the floor. She covered her breasts modestly, but the teasing grin on her face told a different story.

"Am I distracting you enough yet, my Prince?" she asked.

"Drop your hands," he said. Lately, it seemed he needed any distraction he could get.

Nadine laughed and lowered her hands, revealing the pale globes of her full breasts.

"That's better." He gently grasped her wrists and held them above her head, pressing them against the tall wooden column that made up the corner of her four poster bed. "But you mustn't call me Prince."

"I don't care if your father disinherited you," she whispered. "It's a mistake. It will be fixed."

Frederick didn't bother arguing. With the King dead, nothing could be fixed.

He grabbed her scarf from the edge of the bed and wrapped it around her wrists, binding her in place.

"If you aren't a Prince anymore, why couldn't I come to the funeral with you?" Nadine asked. "Am I still your dirty secret, the peasant girl you fuck?"

Frederick responded by slapping his hand hard against her ass. The will hadn't been read until after the King was buried, and that was over a month ago. His stepmother's doing, no doubt.

"I think you've forgotten something," he said.

Nadine laughed and tried to shrug, an impossible motion with her arms so high above her head.

"Do you really still want me, Nadine?" Frederick asked, punctuating each word with another spank. She moaned breathlessly. He ran his finger between her legs, touching her wetness, her desire. "I have nothing now."

"You have me," she gasped.

Frederick opened his breaches and thrust into her from behind, gripping her hips. Nadine grabbed onto the post and moaned with delight. He rammed into her, harder, until he could feel her cunny clench around his cock.

"Oh, yes, Prince Frederick," she cried. "More."

He gave her more, relishing every moment of it, until his climax overtook him and he pulled out, letting his seed spill onto her back, gazing upon her as it dripped down over her reddened ass.

Nadine seemed to believe he was still a Prince, that the enchantress who had married his father wasn't really going to throw him out of the castle. But his stepmother despised him—and nothing would change.

Frederick released Nadine from her restraints, and she collapsed breathlessly into his arms.

"Do you love me, Nadine?"

She gazed up at him in a post-orgasmic haze. "How can I prove it to you?"

He kissed her lips. He considered telling her what she'd forgotten, but reconsidered with a wry smile. "Just...stop calling me Prince. And accept me for what I've become."

Frederick slipped back into the silent castle. Nadine had forgotten it was his eighteenth birthday. When she remembered, he'd punish her for it (hardly a punishment when she always begged for more, but that was Nadine). Time spent with his lover over his lap would be the perfect birthday present.

He certainly wouldn't be getting any presents at home. The grief that still filled the cavernous hall—long after his father's funeral—threatened to close in on him, to suffocate him.

Frederick made it to his suite without arousing any of the servants, and sat on the edge of his bed. No use thinking about getting his old life back. There would be no grand feast to celebrate his birthday this year, nor any year thereafter. His stepmother had poisoned the King's heart against him, and there was no way to undo the damage she had done.

How ironic that Frederick had been disinherited so any child the King had with his stepmother would become the next in line for the throne—and yet she'd never given his father a child. Now his father was dead, and Frederick couldn't even properly mourn him.

Hard to mourn a man who never spoke to him, who believed in his heart that Frederick—at the tender age of four—had been the cause of his mother's death.

Frederick picked up his journal, determined to jot down that evening's sexual adventure. Determined to get rid of the images coursing through his mind. Images of his mother drowning to save his life.

His father was right about him. Frederick growled and shook his head, staring at the words scrawled on the page before him.

Just write. Forget. Escape.

A knock sounded on his dressing chamber door.

"Leave me alone," he said.

Ignoring him, his stepmother opened the door, reclining seductively against the doorframe. "Now, now, that's no way to speak to your mother, darling."

Frederick didn't bother correcting her, even though the word *Stepmother* was on the tip of his tongue. He looked away, not wanting to see her low-cut dress, or the way she ran her long, pale fingers through her jet-black hair as she stared at him.

"Your diary can't be more intriguing than me, now can it?" she teased. She stepped inside his room, closing the door behind her. "Not to a boy who's all grown up."

The beautiful enchantress smiled and stood in front of him, her breasts at his eye-level, since he hadn't stood when she entered. His own personal form of civil disobedience.

The journal flew from his hands by an invisible force, and he gasped.

"Pay attention to me," she commanded.

"I have nothing to say to you. Get out."

"I've been waiting for your birthday, darling," she whispered in his ear, her breath hot against his cheek. "I think you'll enjoy your present."

With a lascivious smile, she pushed her dress down lower, revealing her dark pink nipples.

Frederick turned his head, not wanting to see. "I'm not interested."

His stepmother pointed her finger at him, and just like that, his clothing ripped right off his body, leaving him naked next to his fine cotton suit. He looked down in shock—the garments were torn to shreds.

"Much better," she laughed. "It's getting interesting now, isn't it?"

Frederick clasped his hands over his privates to cover himself. What in God's name was this witch doing?

"You're out of your mind," he growled.

"Oh, come on, don't be a cry baby. I want to see you. All of you." She grinned and snapped her fingers.

His bed sheets pulled off his bed, almost throwing him to the floor. But then the edges of the sheet wrapped around his wrists, binding him, his nakedness exposed.

"Leave me be!" he shouted.

She ran her hand down his body, reverently touching his flesh. "My husband is gone," she whispered. "You're all I have left."

"I won't warm your bed in his place," he said. "I don't want anything to do with you. I'd rather take my chances on the streets."

Frederick shut his eyes, certain that she would try to hypnotize him into desiring her. Her cold hand caressed his cock, and he shuddered.

He expected her to ravish him, using her enchantments to hold him against his will. Instead, she burst into tears.

"Wh-what?" he asked, looking up at her in surprise. "Why are you crying?"

His stepmother shook her head, a furious expression on her face. "Because you hate me so much."

"I don't hate you," he lied. "I just don't want to sleep with you."

"Don't you love me?" she asked, sounding needy, child-like. "Even a little?"

"No, Stepmother. Not even a little."

"Fine," she said, throwing her hands up in anger.

The bed sheets released him, and he sat up, rubbing his wrists.

His stepmother glared at him. "Don't think I don't know about that harlot you visit. She doesn't love you either. Disinherited, not even a real Prince anymore—the only reason she lets you fuck her is because you're so damn *handsome*." She spat the word like it was a curse.

Frederick didn't respond, surprised his stepmother knew about his dalliances. She must have read his private journal entries. He wrote everything in that journal. *Everything.* Including how he felt about his stepmother.

"If you weren't handsome—if you didn't have that perfect, hard young body—no one would ever love you," she said.

"That's not true," Frederick said. "It's *you* no one will ever love! I hate you—"

She glared at him with fire in her eyes.

"—and if you hadn't enchanted my father," he whispered, "he would have hated you as well."

The room went dark, the sconces on the wall all blew out at once by a strong wind. Goosebumps rose on his naked flesh, the hairs on the back of his neck standing up on end.

"You hate me?" She laughed, a manic sound that bubbled up from her throat. "You're not the only one who can hate. You are a beast, and now the whole world will know it!"

Outside his window, lightning flashed and thunder boomed with a ferocity that made him jump in terror. All the while, his stepmother cackled.

Pain tore through him. It felt as if every bone in his body broke and rebuilt, knitting itself back together. His mouth hurt, he'd bitten his tongue and could taste the coppery blood on his lips.

"You. Are. A BEAST!" she screamed.

Frederick fell to the stone floor in agony. He raised his hand to keep her from hurting him, but…his hand…

Oh dear Lord in Heaven

His hand was gone. In its place was a huge animal…paw? No—a gorilla's hand, black and covered in fur.

"What have you done to me?" he cried. Even his voice sounded different. Thick, rumbly, like a lion's roar speaking human words.

The storm stopped. The room lit up with a soft glow from the candles in the sconces. His stepmother gazed at him thoughtfully, as if her anger dissipated once her spell had been cast.

"You have a mirror, see what I've done to you for yourself, *Beast.*"

Frederick tried to rise, but everything still hurt, so he crawled on all fours to the large mirror in the corner of his room. He roared in fright at what he saw.

The animal before him—it couldn't be him, could it? A fearsome combination that didn't exist in nature. His face only slightly resembled his own—he recognized his eyes—still green, still his. His cheekbones, and his jaw. But he had huge fangs, like a tiger. A mane, like a lion. And his body—what was he? A mix of man and gorilla, ten feet tall when he rose up on his hind legs, trying to get a better look. Muscles covered every inch him, not quite hidden by brown and black fur.

His thick, muscular arms hung heavy and low like a gorilla's, but his legs had been transformed into those of a wolf's. He had a tail! Dear God, he had a tail. He was hideous.

Frederick cried out in fear and anger, lashing out at his stepmother with a desperate swipe of his humongous gorilla hand.

"Serves you right," she said, jumping gracefully out of his reach. "I sure hope you were right about your little girlfriend loving you for who you really are. Because until someone falls in love with you—true love—despite your monstrous appearance—you will stay a beast."

"Why?" he asked, crouching on the floor in front of the mirror. "Why?"

"Because you broke my heart," the enchantress said softly.

Frederick inhaled deeply. "No. I mean…" He paused, unsure if he should ask her, afraid it would make her change the rules of her spell. "I mean, why make it so the spell can be so easily broken, when Nadine tells me she loves me?"

She paused, sighing. "I didn't make it that way on purpose, it's just how it is. True love conquers all." Reaching down, she patted his mane like he was a good dog. "It's quite adorable that you really think that harlot will still love you when she sees you as a beast. She won't."

Frederick rose up to his full height, all ten feet of it, and screamed for her to leave him alone.

It came out as… a roar.

Later that night, Frederick prowled through his chambers, afraid to leave lest someone in the court decided to shoot him down out of fear.

His clothing didn't fit, and despite the full coat of fur covering his body, he felt naked and too much like the beast he'd become.

"I need some pants," he murmured to himself.

He couldn't go to see Nadine without clothing. His cock had grown in proportion to his new, huge body, and hung lewdly whenever he stood. And he had to see her so she could break the spell.

Something shifted in the air. He turned to his bed, and lying next to the shredded clothing his stepmother had torn from him while he was still in human form…were pants. Large pants, with a hole for a…tail?

"What the hell is going on?" he wondered.

A piece of paper appeared on the bed, next to the pants. He

tried to pick it up, but only succeeded in swatting at it with his new hand. Sighing, he leaned forward to read the spidery handwriting that sprawled across the note.

~~~

Ask and ye shall receive, Beast. The castle will comply, since no one else will.

All my best,
Your beloved Stepmother

~~~

Frederick growled and pulled the pants off the bed. But he didn't know how to use his new appendages. The claws on his feet ripped everything, and though his animal hands had opposable thumbs, learning to use his new body was going to take some time. And he didn't have time. It was useless.

"I need the damn pants *on* me," he yelled at the empty room.

The pants moved as if of their own accord, pulling up onto his wolves' legs, buttoning themselves. He looked in the mirror.

Well, I look like an animal in clothing. Wonderful. He frowned, but the Beast in the mirror revealed the expression as a horrific grimace with fangs. He tried to smile, to see if that was any better, but it was worse.

How would he ever convince Nadine that he was really himself?

His eyes. They were still human. That girl had stared into his eyes for hours when they made love. They'd spent many nights with her tied up to her bed, gazing at each other as he entered her. Surely she'd know it was him.

He was still himself, on the inside. Since she loved him

(if she loved him)

then she would know it was still him. His life depended on it.

Frederick waited until the middle of the night, when everyone in the castle would be asleep. He crept out of his room, past the ballroom, and went into the grand foyer and out the door. It was a long way to town. Normally he wouldn't risk taking the shortcut through the woods at night because of the wolves, but now he felt quite certain that if anything, the wolves would be afraid of *him*.

Running was faster on all fours. He sprinted through the forest, actually enjoying the way his body responded when he ran. He'd never felt so big and strong in his life.

The lights were out in Nadine's father's house, as he expected they would be. But her room had a door to a balcony, and she always left it unlocked so he could visit her. Hopefully she'd left it unlocked, even though he'd already taken her once today.

Climbing the tree to her balcony was easier in animal form than it had been as a human. The muscles in his new body were incredibly strong. He pounced onto her balcony from the tree and hovered outside the door, panting.

He had to make her understand, *before* she saw him. Or he was doomed.

Let the door be open, he prayed.

It was. Perhaps Nadine had remembered it was his birthday after all.

Frederick slipped inside her bedroom and covered her eyes with his heavy hand, taking care not to scratch her pretty face with the unkempt gorilla finger nails.

"Nadine," he whispered.

The girl whimpered. "Who are you?"

"It's me, it's—" His voice sounded different, though, coming from his new vocal cords. He tried to tell her what happened with the enchantress, but the words wouldn't come out. It just sounded like angry growling.

My stepmother is an evil witch who turned me into a beast. If you love me the spell will be broken.

That's what he kept trying to say, but the words literally could not come out. That witch had cast a spell to keep him from telling people what she'd done!

It's only a spell, I'm still in here, I'm still Prince Frederick!

But only growls emerged from his mouth.

Nadine struggled, pushing his paw away from her face. Her eyes widened in terror, her mouth fell open in a gasp,

"Please, Nadine—"

I am Frederick!

Fuck.

"Look at my eyes," he said, grateful when the words came out. "You know me."

Nadine screamed at the top of her lungs. "Help me, Father! Help!"

Frederick heard the clomping of feet down the hall. He dove out of her room and into the tree, jumped to the ground, and ran.

"Help!" she screamed.

He spared one last glance up at the girl he thought loved him. The girl who didn't even recognize his eyes, his soul.

She howled in fear, and he ran away, back into the woods.

He could still hear her words, echoing in his ears.

"It's a BEAST!"

1

A STRANGER CALLS
(TEN YEARS LATER)

The Beast—for that was what he was now, no longer Prince Frederick—stood at the large bay window and stared out onto the empty landscape surrounding his abandoned castle. A storm raged through the sky, pouring rain down in heavy sheets of water.

It reminded him of the storm on the night he was turned into the Beast.

His stepmother had left that night, ten years ago, after she'd enchanted him and the castle. She took all of the servants with her. Beast pitied the next unfortunate fool who fell under her spell like his father had done.

"I would like a fire," he commanded, pointing to the large stone fireplace.

It immediately lit up, creating a warming glow. Beast sat before it and watched the flames dance. The scent of roses from an open window drifted through his drawing room, and he ordered the window to shut to keep out the rain. Pity it would also keep out the intoxicating scent of roses as well. The thorny bushes were under every window to deter thieves, but Beast loved them for their roses. They provided the only beauty he'd seen in ten long years.

He couldn't even bear to cut the blossoms, for fear of killing their beauty.

BANG.

Beast jumped in his chair. What was that? The front door—

Banging.

No one had come to the castle since his stepmother left. He had a suspicion she had cast a spell over the town so that they'd forget it even existed. That *he* existed.

BANG. BANG.

They'd come—he'd lived in fear that at some point the townspeople would come to slay the Beast. But now he welcomed it. What was living, if he was forced to live his life alone in this vast, empty castle? Unable to seek out human contact. Unable to do anything other than wish for a girl to come along and break the spell.

But the castle's enchantment didn't work that way. When he was hungry, a meal appeared before him. When he wanted a bath, one was magically poured. But there was no response when he wished for company. He knew, he'd tried.

"Fire, go out," he grumbled under his breath. The room fell into darkness once more, and Beast hid in the shadows, awaiting the fate of the stranger knocking on his door.

"Please, may I come in?" a man's voice called. "I'm lost and there were wolves at my heels—waiting for me at the castle gate. I beg you, let me in."

To Henry Castelle, the merchant standing before the intimidating castle door, the only thing that kept him banging on that door was the sure knowledge that if he didn't get shelter tonight, he would die in the woods.

"Please," he called, "I mean you no harm, for the love of God, please let me in!"

The door creaked open. Henry gasped in relief and entered, quickly shutting the door behind him. He looked up gratefully to thank his host, but no one was there.

"H-hello?" he called. "My name is Henry Castelle, I apologize for the intrusion."

His voice echoed off the high ceilings, bouncing back at him. The castle appeared to be deserted.

"If I might warm myself by your fire and spend the night, I will be eternally grateful," he said. To no one.

To his surprise, a fire shot up in the fireplace, the warmth drawing him in closer. An empty chair sat in front of the fireplace, and he sat down, sighing with relief as the chill slowly seeped out of his bones.

What made the fire start, in an abandoned castle?

"Thank you, good fairies, for being so accommodating to a poor stranger such as myself."

No answer.

His stomach rumbled loudly. Henry laughed, his nervousness coming through despite his best efforts. "Sorry, how embarrassing. I'm quite hungry."

It felt strange, talking to what he could only assume were benevolent fairies, but when a tray piled high with food and hot chocolate appeared before him, any strangeness he felt disappeared.

He touched the food gingerly with the fork, afraid it would disappear into thin air the same way it had arrived. But the food was real, as real as his hunger. Henry ate voraciously.

Taking the last sip of chocolate, and feeling sufficiently warmed by the fire, he stood and began to explore a bit.

"If there is a bed where I might spend the night, I would be very grateful," he said aloud to the fairies. "I'll be on my way in the morning."

A glimmer of light caught his eye. Candles lit by themselves along the walls of one corridor, and Henry tentatively followed the path they set out for him.

One room's door was ajar. He peeked in, and seeing a freshly made bed and a warm fire glowing in the fireplace, took off his boots and laid down. With a full belly and the nightmare of his ordeal in the woods behind him, Henry fell asleep the moment his head hit the soft satin pillow.

The following morning, a tray with coffee and fresh fruit awaited him. His clothing, which had been soaked through in the storm the night before, was dry and hanging in the open armoire.

"Fairies, you have outdone yourself," he said. "Thank you so much, you've saved my life. I'll be leaving now."

He finished his breakfast and dressed quickly, not wanting to overstay his welcome. His daughter Belle would be amazed when he told her how he'd spent the night, and he couldn't wait to tell her all about it. If only he'd been able to bring home the riches he'd promised her.

When he'd heard word that one of his lost merchant ships had been found, he had gone off, expecting his wealth to be returned to him. But no such luck. It was almost as if Belle knew, and didn't want to put undue pressure on him. While he had promised to bring her back anything her heart desired—a gown, pearls, gold—his sweet Belle only asked him to bring her back a rose, since she was exceedingly fond of them, and they didn't grow well for her.

Now he couldn't even bring home a simple rose.

Henry sighed and made his way out of the castle, once again thanking the fairies for their hospitality. A large shadow swooped past him in the corner, making him jump in fright, but no one was there.

The castle looked different in the sunshine than it did at

night. The wolves were gone, as was the rain. Droplets glimmered on the beautiful rose bushes that bloomed under every window.

Roses!

Henry leaned into the bush, inhaling the heady scent of the blooms. Carefully, he reached down and plucked a perfect bud from the thorns.

ROARRRRR!

Henry fell to the ground with fright, the rose falling from his hand. Looming above him, growling ferociously with fangs bared, stood a...a *beast*.

"How dare you steal my roses!" the Beast thundered. "After the hospitality I've shown you. I took you in, gave you a fire and food and a warm bed. How do you repay me? By stealing the only beautiful thing I have left!"

Henry's entire body shook with terror. "P-please, sir, I thought the castle was abandoned. I only took the rose because my daughter Belle loves them so much that she asked me to bring her one when I returned home."

The Beast stilled, glaring at Henry. "You have a daughter."

"Y-yes, sir. I meant no harm. I'll return the rose." He hastily attempted to set the flower back onto the bush, yelping when his hand got caught on a thorn.

"You can't return a cut bloom," Beast growled. "It will wither and die. And for that, so must you."

Henry tried to fight but it was no use, not against the Beast's immense size and strength. The Beast opened his mouth wide, revealing horrific fangs, and came closer.

He will devour me, the merchant despaired.

But instead, the Beast bit down onto the back of the man's shirt and dragged him back into the castle, taking no notice of the way the man's body was battered against the hard stone floors.

They went down a narrow staircase, to the dungeon. Chains

17

hung on the walls, and along the floor. The Beast threw him into the corner by a pile of hay, and said, "Chain him."

To Henry's horror, the chains on the floor crept around his ankles and locked in place, capturing him.

"Please, sir, I beg you," Henry said. "Let me see my daughter one last time, and I will return to you."

The Beast laughed at his proposition. "Why should I trust a thief to willingly come back to me, once you are freed?"

"Please, I just…I just want to see my daughter. I want her to know what happened, or she'll never stop worrying about how I disappeared."

"If I let you go see your daughter one last time," Beast said, "and you betray my trust and do not return…I will go into town, hunt you down, and I will eat Belle—like the Beast I am."

The merchant paled. "I could never allow that to happen, sir. Please, let me go, and you have my word I will return."

The Beast nodded, and the chains around the man's ankles unlatched.

"Go now," he roared. "Before I change my mind!"

Back at the merchant's house, Belle Castelle wiped her hands on her apron and stepped back out onto their tiny front porch, shielding her eyes from the sun to see if her father was heading down the road yet.

He shouldn't have been gone so long. Her father was due home yesterday. What could have kept him? Perhaps the storm forced him to spend the night at an inn?

Finally, she saw him in the distance, running toward her. He had no packages, which could only mean that his ship hadn't brought back the wealth he'd been hoping for.

Belle smiled and waved, glad now that she asked only for a rose.

"Belle!" her father gasped, running into her open arms. He hugged her tightly.

"I was worried, Papa," she said. "Are you…are you all right?"

"No," he whispered. "Something horrible happened."

Belle looked at him, frightened. "What, Papa?"

"I never should have taken that rose," he wailed.

Her stomach dropped at his words. "Tell me what happened."

"There's a beast, Belle. A horrible, enormous beast, and if I don't go back to his castle as his prisoner…he's going to eat you." The man sobbed as he said the last part, overcome with emotion.

"Don't worry, Papa. Let's go straight to the Constable and let him know. They will take care of this Beast for us," Belle said.

They ran to the Constable and found him dozing in his chair.

"Sir," Belle coughed, waking him. "We have a problem. My father is being threatened by a Beast who intends to eat me if he doesn't go to his castle as his prisoner."

The Constable looked at the man, at the crazed fear in his eyes, and at the girl. "Very well, my child, I'll take care of everything." He stood and walked into the back room.

"See, Papa? I told you, everything will be fine."

But when the Constable returned, he brought with him his wife Mrs. Sharone, the old lady who ran the Institution for Lunatics.

"A Beast, you say?" she asked dryly.

"Yes, ma'am, a huge beast, with the body of a gorilla, the mane of a lion, and the feet and tail of a wolf!" The merchant nearly fainted in terror just from describing him. "He'll eat Belle alive if I don't go to his castle!"

"Tell me about this castle," she said, picking up a pen and her clipboard. She scrawled a quick note and looked up.

"It's quite large, very old," her Papa described. "And it has fairies that can give you whatever you wish for." Henry paused. "That part was really lovely, actually. But then the Beast came and locked me in his dungeon."

The old lady turned to the Constable. "As you said, Constable. Delusions, hallucinations. I'll take him in to assess whether he's a danger to himself or others."

"You can't!" Henry cried. "If I don't return, he'll eat Belle!"

Belle looked at her father with concern. Was it as Mrs. Sharone said, that he was suffering from delusions?

Her father grabbed her hand and ran out the door with her. "Go back home. I must go to the Beast so he doesn't harm you."

"It must be a misunderstanding," she said. "You only meant to take a rose for me. You're no thief. Surely this...Beast will understand, when I explain."

Her father stared at her in horror. "Absolutely not. You're not going anywhere near that animal."

Belle raised her eyebrows. "I will be accompanying you back to that castle with or without your blessing, Papa. Perhaps hearing your side of the story from a woman will soften the Beast's heart enough to let you go."

They headed back into the woods, hand in hand. Belle wasn't sure what she feared more...finding out her father was indeed suffering from delusions and hallucinations...or finding the Beast.

"This is it," Belle's father whispered, staring at the tall wrought iron gate. "Please, dearest, go home so I can die knowing you are safe."

Belle shook her head. Her father held many strange beliefs, and she'd never seen proof of any of them. Misplaced items around the cottage were not proof of pixies, as much as her father insisted that was so. If the lady who ran the Institution was right about his delusions, Belle needed to know.

"I insist on meeting this Beast myself, Papa," she said quietly. "You can't dissuade me."

"Belle, I—I demand you leave here at once."

Belle shook her head. She was nearly twenty years old now, not a little girl.

Her father sighed at her disobedience and pushed the gate open, shuddering when it creaked. "He's expecting me. I suppose we should get this over with."

They walked up the path to the front door. Belle lifted her hand to knock, but it opened by itself.

"Hello? Is anyone here?" Belle called. Her voice echoed in the cavernous front hall.

A roar shook the stone floor, and Belle jumped in fright, grabbing her father's shoulders.

"He's downstairs," Henry said ominously. "In the dungeon."

"Lord in Heaven," Belle whispered.

Her father inhaled a shaky breath. "I'll go down. You stay here."

"I'll do no such thing," Belle said.

A narrow staircase led down in to the bowels of the castle, and Belle stuck close to her Papa as he descended the stairs.

"I've returned as promised, Beast," Henry called.

They pushed open a heavy door and entered the dungeon. Belle blinked, trying to adjust to the darkness. Something...some *thing* was in the corner, hidden in the shadows.

"Who's there?" she called, her voice sounding high and frightened to her ears.

A beast crept out of the corner on all fours. When he stood, he towered over them both by four or five feet. Belle gasped at the terrifying sight.

"This must be Belle," the Beast said. "The girl who loves roses."

Belle nodded, trembling. "Sir, please don't punish my father for my mistake. I never should have asked for a rose. He didn't mean to steal one, he only meant to please me—"

The Beast roared, silencing her.

Tears stung her eyes. Her father wasn't crazy—this was real. The Beast, he was real! And even more horrible than even her father's story could have prepared her for.

"I won't punish your father then," Beast said. "I will punish you."

Her father threw himself protectively in front of her. "You wanted me, Beast, and I am here as promised. Take me."

Belle couldn't let her father die for her. She couldn't. Henry Castelle was the only truly good soul she knew, and she would protect her Papa to the death.

"Beast," she whispered. "Sir. Take me in his place."

The Beast looked at her appraisingly, staring at her so intently she felt the heat from his gaze.

"You will stay as my prisoner, forever, in place of your father?" Beast asked softly.

"I will." Belle's cheeks were wet with tears, tears for the loss of her freedom, and for the pain she knew she was causing her Papa. But anything was better than having the Beast take him.

"So be it," the Beast said. He turned to her father. "Get out and never return. If you do, or if you send anyone looking for me, I will eat her."

Henry cried out in horror, not moving, reaching his hands toward Belle.

"I said LEAVE!" the Beast roared.

A gale-force wind blew down the stairs, wrapped around her Papa, and carried him out of the dungeon.

"What's happening?" Belle gasped. "Where's my Papa?"

"He has been escorted off the castle grounds," the Beast said.

Belle sobbed, putting her face in her hands. She didn't want to see the Beast, didn't want to see the cold dark dungeon where she would surely die.

"Are you…are you going to eat me?" she asked.

The Beast bared all his fangs, and she trembled.

"No, Belle, I will not be eating you tonight. Get some rest."

Belle worked up the courage to speak again. "Where will I sleep?"

Suddenly, the Beast loomed above her. The muscles across his fur-covered chest bulged, his shoulders so broad they blocked her view of anything but…him.

"There's some hay in the cell. You'll sleep there—unless you planned on sleeping in my bed. I assumed you were the virtuous maiden type. Perhaps I was mistaken."

Belle looked at him in confusion. "No! I mean, I am. But…you're an animal. You don't see me like that, do you?"

Good heavens, where did that even come from? Why was she even entertaining the idea that a beast would want to ravish her?

But something about the way those cool green eyes of his stared at her made her think he wasn't all animal after all. He did speak, and reason, after all. What sort of beast was this?

"I suppose I *am* an animal," he said, his voice thick. "And yes, I see you."

The Beast prowled the great hall above the dungeon. Just below his paws lay a beautiful girl—a girl who would rather die than give her Papa over to him.

Something tugged on his conscience, a nagging feeling of guilt. It wasn't fair to keep her his prisoner. But this was his only chance. The one and only time he'd ever had a girl in his castle, a girl who might be his salvation.

He had to keep her, at least long enough to see if she could ever look past his hideous appearance and into his true soul.

What then? She'd only see the man who'd separated her from her father, the man who'd kept her prisoner. Even if she became accustomed to his beastly appearance, she could never love him.

Accustomed to his appearance…

Yes. That was a start, at least. He would see her often, often enough for her to get used to how he looked, so she wouldn't cringe in fright every time he came by. Once she was able to see him without fear, she'd be able to talk with him.

He already knew they had one thing in common, at least.

They both loved roses.

Perhaps, for her, he could cut some of the deep red blooms. Their color and aroma would brighten the dreary castle up, at least, and might even make her feel more comfortable with her situation.

"Castle," he said to the empty hall. "I want a bouquet of roses in the dungeon for the girl."

Heaven knew she had earned her roses tonight.

Belle laid on a large pile of hay in the cell, staring out the barred window above her head. The window itself was only a foot tall, and seemed to look out onto the grass.

She closed her eyes, determined to imagine herself in a better place. In a beautiful garden filled with roses. She could almost smell them…

The scent of roses in the air became so heady and real that she opened her eyes to see if perhaps everything had been a bad dream. Stone walls surrounded her.

But…where did that bouquet of gorgeous red roses come from? They sat on the edge of her cot, freshly cut and bound together with a ribbon.

Belle reached over and picked the bouquet up, bringing it to her face. They were real, as real as her prison. Had she fallen asleep, had that horrible beast been there to drop them off?

Well, if he brought her roses, maybe he wasn't so horrible.

No. He was horrible. He was keeping her prisoner! And he hadn't even left her any food. Maybe he could run around hunting down deer with those fangs of his, but she needed something on a plate.

"The roses are lovely," she murmured under her breath. "But I can't eat them. I need supper."

Immediately a tray piled high with bread, roasted chicken, and steamed carrots appeared before her. She gasped and jumped back, knocking a piece of bread off the tray in her haste.

"I've gone mad," she breathed. Delusions? Hallucinations?

But the food smelled so good. So…real. How could food that appeared out of thin air be real? Perhaps she was like a person lost in the desert who thinks they see a waterfall, only to find out they are licking a sand dune.

Her hunger got the better of her, and she picked up the bread, holding it close to her face to examine it. It didn't disappear when she touched it, so that was promising.

A tiny bite, as a scientific experiment of sorts, couldn't hurt. Right?

Belle nibbled the bread, waiting for her mind to snap out of it and to discover she was gnawing on the edge of her shoe. That didn't happen, and the bread was extremely tasty, so she moved in for the chicken.

Amazing!

"Thank you for the food," she said to the empty cell.

No response. Fairies? Could it really be fairies helping her, like Papa had told the Constable?

"I'd love some wine, if you're in the giving mood, fairies," she added. Not that she actually thought it would happen. It was merely an experiment.

An open bottle of red wine and a glass settled onto the stone floor. What on earth?

Belle didn't usually drink, but tonight she wanted to escape her cold reality and fall asleep. Perhaps she would wake to find the roses, the food, and the wine were all part of an elaborate dream.

In the meantime, she intended to get drunk.

Belle kneeled on the hard floor and poured herself a glass of wine, carefully taking the glass back onto the hay with her. Was she being granted wishes?

She took a deep sip, relishing the taste. Why had she been such a teetotaler all these years? Wine was delicious. Especially magic wine gifted from fairies.

"If I am being granted wishes, I wish to be home with my Papa."

Nothing. Nothing happened at all.

"I wish for a saw so that I may cut those bars loose," she tried.

Yes! A sharp, scary-looking metal saw appeared at the floor below the window, clattering against the stone.

What would happen if she escaped? The Constable thought her father was crazy; if she said there was indeed a beast, would they want to send her to the Institution for Lunatics as well?

If no one came to slay the Beast, he would no doubt find them and eat them both. Still, she had to try. With an unladylike gulp, Belle finished her glass of wine for courage.

Now she only had to avoid sawing off one of her fingers. She picked up the saw, surprised by how heavy it was. It was a difficult angle, standing on the hay with the saw, but she may as well start somewhere.

"I wish for these bars to be gone," she said. Nothing happened.

The sound of the saw screeching against the metal bars rattled her nerves, and she wasn't making much headway, even after giving it a really good try for about a half an hour. The one bar she was working on wasn't even cut through yet, and she still had five more to go.

It was too much. Her arms ached, and the hay she stood on began to look more inviting as a place to sleep.

At least the saw could be a weapon, for when the Beast returned. She could threaten him with it and demand to be set free.

If he set her free, she would have broken her word, though. And he'd go after her Papa again. That was the whole reason she was there in the first place.

Sudden movement outside the window caught her eye. She glimpsed something outside—a wolf? No. *The Beast.* He prowled along the edges of the forest, and though her vision was limited by the small window, one thing she could see clearly—the moonlight glinting off of his bloody fangs.

It appeared the Beast had been out hunting.

Please, God, let this all be a dream. Please, please, God.

But it wasn't a dream. She was awake, and more terrified of her predicament than even before.

Belle exhaled shakily, and put the saw down, nudging it under the hay a bit with her foot to hide it from view. She poured another glass of wine and sipped from the glass, cradling the roses in her arm, breathing in their comforting scent.

I wish to wake up at home with Papa...

The wine finally hit her, and she was asleep when the Beast returned.

2

THE BEAST'S CAPTIVE

Henry Castelle was sweaty and streaked with dirt from the woods by the time he raced to the Constable.

"You must help me!"

The Constable took his boots off his desk and frowned. "Let me guess. This is about a beast."

"Yes!" Henry gasped. "The Beast has taken Belle prisoner. He could be eating her alive as we speak, we have to save her!"

The Constable nodded. "Let's calm down now, Mr. Castelle. Please sit, I'll be right back. We'll get you the help you need."

Henry slumped into the chair in relief. Finally, they were listening.

But the Constable returned from the back office with his wife Mrs. Sharone. The lady who ran the Institution for Lunatics. Henry grabbed the side of the chair as she approached.

Mrs. Sharone stared down at him in his chair. "A beast has taken your daughter prisoner, is that correct?"

"Yes, madam."

"Is she dead?" She frowned, picking up her clipboard.

"I hope not," Henry whispered. "I don't know. He could have eaten her. We must find her."

"Mr. Castelle," she said, "I think you are overwhelmed and scared. I think you're trying to tell us that something awful happened, and that it wasn't your fault, am I right?"

Henry nodded mutely.

"Mr. Castelle, are *you* the Beast?"

"What? No!"

"Did you hurt your daughter, Mr. Castelle?" she asked.

Henry jumped up. "You're the lunatic, Mrs. Sharone. And if the Constable doesn't help me get Belle and slay this Beast so help me God I will—"

He didn't get to finish his threat. The Constable pushed him to the floor, and he hit his head. Everything went black and fuzzy for a moment. When he came to, his wrists hurt—the Constable had put handcuffs on him.

"Well," Mrs. Sharone said, her voice sounding distant and tinny. "He's certainly a danger to others. I'll take him to the Institution so he can be sedated. I fear the worst for his beautiful daughter."

The Constable nodded grimly. "Henry's covered in dirt. I'll search his garden for any fresh gravesites."

Back at the castle, the Beast entered the dungeon quietly. He wanted to check on the girl, to be sure she was all right.

A half-empty bottle of wine lay on the ground by her hay pile, where she sprawled, asleep. Beast grinned. It amused him that both she and her father knew how to get what they needed from his enchanted castle. Neither of them had needed a note explaining it, the way he had.

That indicated that she was the accepting sort. When things

she asked for appeared out of nowhere, she seemed to have accepted it and moved on, no explanation needed. Hopefully that meant she would learn to accept his appearance as well.

Only time would tell.

The Beast crept toward her, not wanting to frighten her by waking her, as he had done to Nadine that night so long ago. The memory of her screams of terror still filled his nightmares.

Belle's long brown hair splayed around her head, one pale hand nestled under her cheek. Her plain blue dress was simple but form-fitting, as if she'd made it before she'd finished growing into her curves. The buttons at her neck were undone, leaving her collarbone exposed.

She was beautiful…no wonder they called her Belle. The girl certainly qualified to have a name that meant Beauty.

Beast leaned in closer to her, breathing in the warm, sweet scent of her skin. He couldn't recall ever doing that to a girl when he was human—sniffing her. Maybe he had become more of an animal than he'd thought.

Belle stiffened, her brow creasing, her eyes squeezed shut.

"I didn't mean to wake you," Beast said softly.

She kept her eyes closed. "I'm scared," she whispered.

"I won't hurt you."

"Don't eat me."

He smiled but composed himself, knowing a smile only looked like he was baring his fangs. If she chose to open her eyes when he was grinning at her, she'd probably run screaming.

"I won't eat you, Belle," he promised.

He'd never actually eaten a person, but it had seemed like a good threat when Henry Castelle was there. Now he wished he could take it back so she wouldn't be so frightened to have him near her.

"Why are you here, then, if not to eat me?" she asked.

"I wanted to see you," he admitted. "It's been so long since

I've had human contact."

"How long?" she asked, keeping her eyes shut.

"Ten years." He ran his fingers over her silky hair.

"What happened ten years ago?"

He couldn't tell her, so he wouldn't try. "I...changed."

"Change back," she whispered.

If only it were so simple. Perhaps she thought he'd been a nice beast who changed into a mean beast. He laughed, the sound coming out like a howl.

Belle whimpered, and Beast stopped laughing. He touched her cheek gently, running his hand across her smooth face, relishing the feel of her skin. She bit her lip to hold back a gasp.

"I'd like to change," he said. "Maybe you can help me."

"How?"

"It's been a long time since I've had a woman for company," he said. "I want to touch you. Is that all right?"

Belle inhaled sharply, but she nodded.

"Why are you saying yes, if you're afraid?"

"Because you're so big," she whispered, her eyes still shut. "I'm scared you'll hurt me."

"I promise I won't hurt you," he said. "You have my word. My only desire is to make you feel good right now."

At that, she relaxed visibly, the crease leaving her forehead. Beast kept one hand against her cheek, and with his other hand, spanned the length of her body and gently touched her foot.

"Your feet are cold," he said, holding them in one large hand to warm them.

"I am a bit chilled, sir."

"It's cold and dark down here in the dungeon," he admitted. "I think you should have taken me up on my offer to sleep upstairs, in my bed."

Belle moaned as he moved his hand up her leg to her knee, whether in fear or pleasure, he couldn't tell. But she wasn't stopping him.

Her blue dress lifted, leaving her thighs bare. She wore nothing underneath, and he could smell her feminine musk. The scent drove him wild with desire, but he forced himself to go slowly, to not frighten the girl.

Beast rubbed her thighs, warming her flesh. With a sigh, her legs parted ever so slightly, her body melting into the hay.

He reached the junction of her thighs, the one part of her body that threw off heat. His thumb rested on the tender bud he found, more beautiful than any rose in his garden.

"Have you ever been touched here?" he asked quietly, his voice thick.

"No," she whispered. She was wet for him, slippery beneath his hand.

Beast slid one finger inside her tight channel. "You're not a virgin, Belle. How is it that no one has touched you here?"

She gasped, tilting her hips up to meet his fingers, still keeping her eyes shut. "But I *am* a virgin, sir. Well—the baker's apprentice last year…just a little kissing in the barn loft. He didn't know how to do…what you're doing."

"Do you like it?" Beast asked, stilling.

"Please, don't stop," she said, her breath catching.

Beast chuckled. "I didn't ask you if I should stop, Belle. I asked you if you liked it." He quickened his pace, rubbing tight little circles over her bud.

"Yes," she gasped. "Yes, Beast."

With a delicate cry, Belle came, covering his hand in her juices. Since she wasn't looking, Beast brought his hand to his mouth and licked his fingers clean. It was too bad he'd already promised not to eat her, because she was absolutely delicious.

"Look at me, beauty. Look at my eyes."

Belle lids fluttered open and she gazed into Beast's eyes. "I've never seen a beast such as you," she whispered.

"You think I'm a monster."

"That wasn't what I was thinking, sir. I was thinking you look quite…majestic. Like a mythical creature."

The Beast held his smile at bay so as not to frighten her. "Flattery."

She smiled and turned her head, and his hand fell from her face.

"You don't want me to touch you when you can see what I look like, is that right?" he asked. "Do I still scare you, after all that?"

"Any man who kept me captive in a dungeon and then approached me late at night would scare me."

"Well, beauty, that is a good point. But I am not any man." This time he couldn't keep from grinning, all of his fangs bared at her. "I am the *Beast*."

Belle cried out in horror and lashed out at him, cutting deep across his chest with something painfully sharp.

He howled in pain and anger.

What happened? The girl had gone from post-orgasmic to homicidal in short order.

She jumped up, still holding her weapon, hurtling herself past him.

"I'm sorry, Beast," she called as she flew up the stairs out of dungeon.

Beast held his hand over the bleeding wound on his chest. Where had she gotten a weapon? And worse, why had she left him, right when things were starting to get interesting?

He was torn between rushing after her, or letting her go. Perhaps keeping her prisoner was a bad idea.

But it had been a decade since he'd become the Beast, and this was his first—possibly last—opportunity to get to know a woman without having her run screaming.

Which, of course, is exactly what Belle had just done.

The moon shone brightly through the cell window. Nighttime. The wolves would be out.

While he was safe from wolves, little Belle would be in danger. He had to go find her, and worry about whether he'd keep her or not until after she was safe from harm.

She still had her weapon with her...a saw of some sort. When he rescued her, she might cut his head off with the damn thing.

The idea didn't bother him as much as he thought it would. If he couldn't have her, he might as well give up hope of ever changing, and die a Beast.

Belle ran through the cavernous front hall. "Open the door," she cried to the fairies. "Please, open the door!"

The door flew open and Belle tumbled out into the dark night. She ran blindly, her only goal to get as far away from the castle as possible.

"Fairies, I need a horse," she said.

Nothing happened. The fairies were fickle, it seemed. So she ran on.

She'd cut the Beast badly. Was he okay? Her conscience tugged at her, but she tamped it down. She'd had a chance to escape, with him so close and her hand gripping the handle of the saw—so she'd taken it. When he bared his fangs at her, she knew he'd eat her alive, no matter what protestations he made on the matter. Even if he'd done incredible things to her body with those big hands of his.

Cutting him and fleeing was the right thing to do. The *only* thing to do.

Hideous howling and growling surrounded her in the dark forest. She gasped, freezing on the spot, afraid to move lest she betray her location to the Beast.

The growling came closer. Not the Beast—no—wolves!

Belle screamed and swung her saw around her in a circle, trying to make herself as big and threatening as she could. But the wolves knew they outnumbered her. Her frantic posturing did nothing to keep them at bay.

ROARRRRR

Belle turned to the sound behind her. The Beast!

"Get behind me," he roared. "Now."

She scrambled to obey, fearing for her life.

One wolf jumped at the Beast, and he gnashed his teeth, sending it tumbling to the ground. The Beast bared his bloody fangs to the pack, his own growls overtaking those of the wolves.

Finally (*thank the Lord!*) the wolves scampered off into the woods.

Belle gripped the saw in her hands. The Beast swiveled and knocked it from her grasp to the forest floor. She cried out in surprise.

He picked her up, throwing her over his broad shoulder. She screamed again, frightened to be so high up off the ground, and he was moving so fast, sprinting back to the castle.

"Beast, I'm sorry I hurt you," she wailed, certain he was carrying her to her death. But he said nothing in reply.

When they got back to the castle, the Beast set her down in front of him on the stone.

"Are you all right?" Beast asked, his expression filled with concern.

Not what she'd been expecting. "Um…I'm quite all right I think, thank you. I mean…thank you, for saving me."

He grunted.

"I'm…I'm sorry I cut you," she added weakly. "Please don't eat me."

"For the last time, Belle, I will not eat you!"

Belle trembled. "Thank you."

"You deserve to be spanked for pulling a stunt like that," he growled.

She hadn't received a threat like that since she was a child.

"It's not my fault," she said. "You confused me. First you made me feel so...amazing—that thing you did to me—but then you scared me half to death and I —I just want to go home. I can't stay your prisoner forever. I'd rather die."

She looked up, expecting to see anger, but instead, he looked sad.

"You'd rather die than live with me?" he asked softly.

Was this a test? If she answered yes, would he eat her?

"I can't stand the thought of being here forever, and never seeing my Papa again. That's all," she whispered.

"I'm sorry, Belle," he said. "I know what it's like to be imprisoned, to want to be set free."

"Someone...someone imprisoned you?"

"Yes." He paused, as if surprised by his own words. "That's why I need you to stay. Why I can't let you go."

"Please, sir," she said. "I'll do anything if you'll give me my freedom."

The Beast bared his fangs and she cried out.

"I apologize," he said. "That's just...that's what I look like when I smile. No need to fear."

"That's your smile?" she gasped. "I thought you were going to eat me."

Beast shook his head, his mane flowing down his muscular back. "If you say that one more time I will eat you just to shut you up."

When he bared his teeth again, Belle held her ground. "You're smiling again, aren't you?"

"I am."

"Well. So glad my terror amuses you." She crossed her arms

and stared at him defiantly.

"I won't eat you," Beast repeated emphatically. "But you wounded me and you broke your word, you ran away. You could have been killed by those wolves."

"I'm sorry," she whispered, gazing at the bloody laceration across his muscular chest. "Does it hurt?"

"Yes," he said, his voice gruff. "Come here."

Belle stood frozen, afraid to go to him. What would happen?

"Bend over the table," he ordered, pointing to the marble table holding a vase of roses in the middle of the foyer. The cut roses hadn't been there yesterday.

She eyed him warily. "Why?"

"Why do you think, Belle?" He raised his heavy brow, and once again she was shocked to discover how...*human* his beautiful, intense eyes were.

"You're going to spank me," she said softly. "I suppose I deserve it. I thought you were going to kill me for wounding you and running away when you brought me back here. I'd much prefer a spanking if it will put us on friendlier terms."

"Enough talk. You're stalling."

Belle hadn't been spanked in years, and never by a creature who was twice her height and probably four times her weight. Never by a creature, period. His huge hands looked strong and hard.

"Please Beast, don't hurt me," she whispered, leaning over the marble table to brace herself. "I'm sorry I cut you with the saw."

"I fully intend to hurt you, Belle," the Beast said. "But I would never *harm* you. Unlike when you tried to kill me with your saw, I am merely punishing you with a little spanking."

Belle shut her eyes, knowing he was smiling, baring his fangs. She could hear it in his voice. It was almost as if he relished the chance to spank her. His large, warm hands lifted her dress, draping it over her back.

She'd never felt so vulnerable, with her naked bottom bared to the empty room. Not even when he'd played with her most intimate areas had she felt this vulnerable. That at least had been pleasurable. This…this frightened her.

The Beast caressed her ass, and she gasped at the contact.

"Hold still, beauty," he said.

With a hard swat, he spanked her, his hand spanning both cheeks at once.

Belle cried out, more in surprise than pain. Not just pain—humiliation. How dare this Beast treat her like a child?

He spanked her again, harder this time. Heat radiated off her flesh and she knew her skin reddened under his touch.

"Don't run away again," Beast growled, spanking her bare ass faster, building a rhythm that left her breathless, gasping, whimpering.

"I won't, Beast, I swear I won't!" She would swear anything at this point, anything to make him stop. Because now, it hurt. *Hell and damnation* it hurt.

He paused. "You gave me your word when I released your father. How can I trust you now?"

She looked over her shoulder at him, her hands still pressed against the cool marble table. "I don't know. I don't want to be your prisoner…forever."

"Are you suggesting that if there were a time limit, you'd be able to truly give your word, that'd you stay?" Beast asked slowly. "If I didn't ask for forever?"

God, *was he giving her a way out?*

"Yes, Beast. I can tolerate anything if I know I'll be back home soon, if I can hold onto that hope."

Beast bared his fangs, and she cringed.

"Y-you're smiling," she said. It might take her a while to get used to that.

"I am. I have a proposition for you." He gently smoothed her skirt back over burning bottom, and turned her around to face him. "I haven't had a woman in my bed for a very long time. If you'd be willing to sleep with me, I'd reduce your lifetime imprisonment to one short year."

Belle gasped, both at the idea of sleeping with him, and the idea of a life sentence being reduced to a year.

"You'd crush me to death," she said, looking up at his towering hulk.

"I would not. Wasn't I very gentle with you earlier, in your cell, when I made you feel so amazing, as you put it? Right before you—"

Right before she cut him and ran. Yes, she could recall something like that happening.

"It's really not 'willing' if I must bed you for my freedom," she pointed out.

"Forget I said anything," he growled. "I'll see you safely to your cell."

"Wait!" She paused, frantic, not willing to give up her one chance of freedom. And also not willing to give up a very rational excuse for having more experiences like the one he'd given her earlier. "Three months. Then I can go."

"Six months, and you do everything I say."

"It's—It's a deal, Beast." She sighed. "I'm yours for six months. And then you set me free and you forget all about me and my Papa."

Beast smiled. Yes…definitely a smile. "I very much doubt I will ever forget you, beauty. But I'll never harm you."

Her thoughts immediately flew to her sore bottom, at the way he spanked her so thoroughly. Although, it was as he said. He'd hurt her, he had not harmed her. She would remember her punishment when she sat down for a day or two, but it wasn't like he'd crippled her.

Or ate her. That was something to be grateful for.

Beast looked around his castle as though seeing it for the first time. "I suppose, if you'll be staying awhile, we could arrange more suitable sleeping quarters for you."

"In your bed," she guessed.

"You'll have your own suite." He spoke louder, and Belle realized he was probably summoning the fairies. "Belle will need a suite, with a four poster bed, a bath, dresses in the armoire, and a fire ready for her."

"The fairies can do all that?" she asked.

"Fairies?" He shook his head and began to say something, but it just sounded like growling to her.

"Pardon?"

"Never mind. If you'd like to believe we have a fairy infestation, then by all means. Believe what you will." Beast gestured for her to follow him up the stairs and into the west wing of the castle.

She followed, mesmerized by the glorious tapestries and paintings that adorned the long hallways. Where had a beast gotten such wealth?

One oil painting, of a young man, about her age perhaps, caught her eye. His handsome face seemed to draw her in. Belle stopped in front of it, gazing at the portrait.

"He's beautiful," she whispered.

"Thank you," Beast said. "I mean…I'm glad you appreciate the art in my castle."

There was something familiar about the young man's intense green eyes.

"Do I—do I know him?" she asked.

"Perhaps. You would have been a child when this portrait was taken."

She looked at the inscription on the gold plaque beneath the portrait. It said "Prince Frederick," and was dated ten years prior. That would have been when she was nine years old, and certainly never out and about, gazing into handsome princes' green eyes.

"I suppose I don't," she said.

41

For some reason the thought made her sad. What had become of that young man? Perhaps the portrait was from another country. She'd never heard of a Prince Frederick before.

Beast kept walking down the corridor, so she followed.

"I imagine you ate everyone who lived in this castle," Belle said. "That's why they aren't here, and...you are."

Beast whirled around, and she was so caught off guard that she stumbled against his enormous chest.

"I'm sorry," she gasped.

"That is not what happened."

"The painting was ten years ago. Ten years ago, you changed. You told me so. I was merely...taking an educated guess."

"There was nothing educated about it," Beast said. "And if you'll be staying under my roof for the next six months, you might want to reconsider playing guessing games if you want us to get along."

She put her hand to her mouth. "I apologize."

"We're here." He stopped in front of a large door, with the words "Belle's Suite" etched into a small silver placard on the door. "If you need anything—"

"I'll just ask the fairies," she finished for him.

"Um, yes. Exactly."

"Will I be sleeping...uninterrupted?" She blushed as she spoke the words, but she had to know if he'd be taking her up on their deal tonight.

"Dawn is almost here. Sleep as late as you'd like. I won't bother you until you come to me."

"But...what if I *never* choose to...come to you?"

Beast raised his heavy brow. "Your six months begins when you do. Take as long as you need."

He held opened the door to her suite and she stepped inside, reveling at the sight of the large four poster bed with the flowing white linens, the glowing warmth of the fire burning in the fireplace, and most of all...the roses. They were everywhere, the scent beckoning her.

"Good night, beauty."

Belle shut the door behind her, pressing her ear to the wood until she could hear the Beast's heavy footsteps continue down the hall. The suite was far more luxurious than even the home she'd lived in with her Papa, before he lost all of his wealth. She went to the bath, which was already filled with steaming hot water. Rose petals floated on the top of the water.

With a heavy sigh she removed her dress and sank into the tub, grateful for a chance to wash off the insanity of the night so she could start fresh. She smelled like hay from the cell, and had dirt on her legs from falling in the woods. The water soothed her aching buttocks.

That Beast knew how to spank.

She took her time washing herself, washing her hair, and combing it out. When she was done, she slipped on a white nightgown. It fit perfectly.

"Thank you, fairies," she said. She paused. "May I have more wine, please?"

A single glass of red wine appeared. No bottle. Oh well, that would have to do. Hopefully it would put her to sleep and keep her from dreaming about all the terrible, sinful,

wonderful, intoxicating

things that Beast had done to her. And what more might be in store...

3

FREDERICK

In his room down the hall, Beast collapsed onto his bed. The mattress sank in under his massive weight. Had he done the right thing, agreeing to keep Belle only six months? Surely that wasn't enough time to get her to see past his appearance, forgive him for taking her captive, and fall in love with him.

There was too much to accomplish, in too short a time.

Also, the cut on his chest burned like fire.

"I need a washrag and ointment," he said, not bothering to lift his heavy head from the pillow.

The items appeared, and he tended to his wound. But it still hurt like hell.

"Laudanum, please," he said. The opium tincture appeared, and he sipped a bit of the bitter medicine. He took care not to abuse the potent drug, but with a fresh wound, he knew he'd be tossing and turning without it.

His sleep was quiet, dark, and deep. In his dreams, he was no longer a Beast. He was himself. He was Frederick.

And he still had a captive to attend to.

Belle woke gently, or perhaps she didn't wake at all. A light caress ran along her arm.

Beast?

She opened her eyes. It was a man—a man in her room. "Who are you?" she gasped. "What are doing here?"

She bit down on her first instinct—to scream for the Beast to come to her rescue. Doing so wouldn't make much sense, since the last thing she wanted was the Beast in her suite.

The intruder—the man—said nothing, he just looked at her until she recognized him...from the portrait. The beautiful young man with the amazing green eyes.

Just a dream, then. That was good. To dream and know she was dreaming meant she could do whatever she wished, and awake unscathed.

"Hello, beauty," the Prince said, settling next to her on the bed. "I saw you looking at my portrait."

"I did," she whispered, the way she often did in the dark.

Normally, she would be absolutely shocked for a stranger to sit on her bed—but this was only a dream, and so she welcomed it. Welcomed *him.*

"Do you find me handsome?" He kissed her neck, igniting a spark of desire.

Just a dream...none of mattered if it wasn't real.

"Yes." Boldly, she reached out and touched his clean-shaven face, and stared into his eyes. Familiar eyes.

"Is that very important to you?" he asked.

What a strange question! "I don't know," she murmured. "I *am* glad you're here. It's nice to see another person, if only while I sleep."

"My name is Frederick."

"Frederick… Am I being haunted?" she asked.

Because while he was touching her, running his hands over her body, ahh…it didn't feel so much like a dream. It felt real. It felt… incredible. Did ghosts feel real?

"In a way, perhaps I am haunting you," Frederick said. "Don't be afraid. The Beast is good. He didn't eat me, Belle, if that's what you think."

"Are you imprisoned here, in the castle?" she asked. "Like me?"

Frederick smiled. "I am."

She wrapped her arms around his neck and drew the handsome Prince onto her, relishing the weight of his body on hers. Surprising that she could feel the weight of a ghost, or a dream, or whatever Frederick was.

"One moment," she gasped, sitting up. "Are you actually a prisoner in this castle, and did you find me, and are you about to ravish me? Or am I dreaming?"

"Yes." Frederick smiled, beautiful straight white teeth that didn't frighten her exactly—not the way Beast's fangs did.

"Y-yes?"

"Yes, to all of it." Frederick kissed her long and deep, his tongue dancing with hers.

Belle moaned with passion as his kisses left her lips, traveling down her neck, to her breasts. She tore at her nightgown to give him better access.

She only prayed this was really a dream.

Who cares?

She was a captive—none of it would be her fault, surely. When she got back home she'd just pretend none of it happened. As long as she was enjoying the experience, why deny herself?

And oh my goodness, she was enjoying herself.

"Belle," Frederick whispered, his breath hot against her nipple. "You must try to love the Beast. Don't be so afraid of

47

him."

"I could never love the Beast, Frederick," she said. "Never."

Frederick sucked her nipple into his mouth and she gasped in delight. No one had ever done that to her before. The feeling was…otherworldly.

"That disappoints me," Frederick said. His mood seemed to darken. "I should…I should go."

"I can't change my answer," she said. "But will I see you again?"

"If I'm to survive, yes," he said. "Please, Belle. Go to the Beast. Don't be afraid."

"He—" she blushed, unsure if she could reveal what had happened, even to a ghost. Or a dream-man. Or a prisoner in the castle intent on making her think she was insane. *Whomever* the handsome man with his mouth on her breast was.

"The Beast *spanked* me, Frederick. Like a naughty child. It was humiliating."

Frederick grinned. "You're looking at it the wrong way."

Belle frowned. "Is there any other way to look at it?"

Frederick dropped his hand to her ass, caressing the tender skin through her nightdress. "I think he quite enjoyed the experience. Having that luscious bottom under his hand, watching it pink up with heat."

Belle laughed. "I could imagine *you* enjoying yourself, then."

"There are ways to enjoy submitting to the Beast. Don't be so frightened of new experiences." He gave her bottom a firm squeeze, and she gasped. "Perhaps when you're healed, you'll allow me to spank you. I'll make you love it."

"I don't see how that's possible," she said, but it was a lie.

The desire in his eyes aroused her. Yes, perhaps she'd allow Frederick to spank her. It was just a dream, after all.

It was, wasn't it?

The following morning, Belle couldn't find the plain blue dress she'd arrived in. But the armoire was filled with glorious gowns, the sort of dress she'd never worn, out of modesty. It didn't seem right to be bedecked in jewels and pearls and lace when she rode in her wagon past children begging on the streets.

Of course, that was in another life. Before Papa lost everything. Perhaps if she'd agreed to buy the dresses when she had the chance, she would have been able to sell them later. Instead, they moved to the country and she wore even plainer clothes than before.

Wearing something plain didn't look like an option right now.

Belle picked a stunning pale pink dress from the armoire and dressed, calling on the fairies to help lace her up, and to pin her hair.

She had to find the other prisoner, Frederick. Last night had felt too real for him to be just a dream (in which case, she had behaved shockingly inappropriately). Or if it was a dream, surely that dream was meant to inspire her to find him.

She tip-toed down the hallway, pausing only to look at the handsome Prince's portrait. Heat warmed her cheeks at the memory of his touch. Silly to blush from a dream.

(was it really a dream?)

Where was the Beast? Every corner she turned, she feared she'd run into him. That he'd ask her if she was ready to…begin.

I'll never be ready. The Beast frightened her almost as much as the strange desire he aroused in her, whenever he looked at her from his towering height.

But Frederick had implored her to go to the Beast. If only she could find Frederick, she could figure out what was going on.

She knocked softly on every door she passed, praying at each one that it wouldn't be the Beast's room. The handsome young man couldn't be in the dungeon, because she'd already been there, and had felt frightfully alone. So he must be living in the castle, somewhere.

"Fairies," she whispered. "Show me the way to Frederick's room."

A candle on the wall lit, and she turned to it in surprise. With the sunlight streaming in through the windows of the castle, she certainly hadn't been expecting candlelight.

To the right, another candle.

Belle followed their lead, walking in the direction of each newly flaming wick. The fairies had led her to a closed door at the end of wing.

Shivers of anticipation rushed through her. If Frederick was indeed beyond that door, would he know her? Or had her dream been a vision of which he played no part?

Carefully, Belle pushed open the large wooden door. It creaked on its hinges from years of disuse.

"Prince Frederick?" she whispered.

No reply.

The room was clearly a young man's room, and well-appointed. Glass shards covered the floor. Belle skirted around them. A long, floor-length mirror stood in the center of the room, the looking-glass smashed to pieces. The violence of the act left a thrumming vibration in the room, it seemed.

"Frederick, are you here?" she asked again.

No reply.

Of course. Her over-active imagination at work, once again. But then, why did the fairies lead her here, if Frederick didn't exist?

She crossed the room, stepping over the broken glass, and sat on the bed. The sheets were askew, as if no one had bothered to straighten them after some...some sort of struggle.

Belle smoothed the sheets into place, and uncovered a leather-bound book.

A book!

Having something to read would help her pass the time, and hopefully make the next six months go by quicker.

She just needed to give herself to the Beast so her six month sentence could start. But how?

I can never—

—don't think about that now. Just read. Escape.

The book's yellowing, aged pages were all handwritten. A diary, perhaps.

She opened it to the first page.

The Journal of HRH Prince Frederick, to be read by no one.

Belle smiled. Goodness, that sounded almost like how she'd started her diary as well, when she was a teenager.

Settling back onto the satin pillow, Belle turned the page, and read.

~~~

None of the women at Court want to play the games I wish to play. Lady Amelia is almost as old as I, sixteen, and yet she only wants to steal kisses, then giggle with her friends when they see me ride by.

I finally got Amelia alone in the wine cellar, but she guarded her virginity with more ferocity than Father's men guard the castle gate. My attempts to woo her resulted in nothing more than me getting a slap across the face with her glove.

I told her I'd like to use that glove on her, perhaps on her cheeks (I touched her derriere to let her know exactly what I meant), but she gasped as if I'd suggested murdering her, and ran away. I do believe I will cease courting her.

~~~

Belle laughed out loud. She could only imagine the look on the Lady Amelia's face when the young Prince requested to spank her. It probably looked a bit like the expression on her own when the Beast told Belle to bend over.

From the looks of it, Prince Frederick had quite a taste for tying girls up and spanking them. But only if they were willing. Belle flipped through pages of entries, each detailing his pursuit and failure to entice dozens of young ladies into his bed.

~~~

Surely it is my Stepmother's doing, that no girl will have me. A spell of some sort. Heaven knows she has enchanted the King to do her bidding. It is as if no one recognizes that when my father is gone, I will be King, and the woman of my choosing will be Queen. That when I marry (if I marry), the woman I choose will be a Princess until I ascend to the throne.

None of that is apparent. It can only be black magic to cloud the Court's minds against the subject. A rumor has gone around that my Stepmother gave birth to a demon that died at birth. My father won't comment on the matter. Can't he see she's using her magic to give him an heir, when God Himself doesn't want her to spawn a child?

Why does he need an heir, when he has me? Aren't I enough?

~~~

Belle had no memory of a King, or a castle, or an Enchantress Queen or a Court or any of the things Prince Frederick wrote of in his journal. Was it all just the imaginative musings of a teenage boy, wishing his life were more interesting than it was?

Or was it…real?

Clearly, the castle was real. The portrait of Prince Frederick was real. The castle did have some sort of…something, happening. Fairy infestation.

Could it be that this evil Queen had "clouded" everyone's memories, as the journal suggested?

Either way, Belle could empathize with the young man's feelings. She too felt like she wasn't enough, at times. The only daughter to her Papa, a poor consolation when they were forced to move out of town and into the country to work for a living.

Her stomach grumbled rudely, interrupting her thoughts.

"Fairies," she said. "I would like some breakfast, please, and tea."

She sat up on the bed, awaiting the tray that would be magically appearing, but none came.

"Fairies?" she asked. "Are you through granting wishes?"

A note fell on her lap, settling against the luxurious pale pink fabric of her dress.

Belle picked it up, eyeing it warily.

~~~

Please do me the honor of joining me in the main dining hall for Breakfast.
With Devotion,
The Beast.

~~~

She dropped the note to the bed with a gasp. The handwriting...it was larger, more heavily scrawled, yes, but it was so...similar, somehow. One could almost imagine the Beast studied the handwriting in Prince Frederick's journal. Or perhaps it was something else?

Belle picked up the note and used it as a bookmark to mark her place in the journal, and hid it in the folds of her gown. None of this made sense. She'd need to study it further later, when she was alone.

Right now, it was time to dine with the Beast.

Belle took deep, calming breaths as she navigated the immense castle to meet with the Beast. It was only breakfast, after all. The Beast has promised her that she could be the one to let him know if—when—she was ready to take things to the next level.

The more...intimate level.

Perhaps she could close her eyes and imagine the Beast was Frederick. It probably wouldn't work, considering the sheer size of the Beast and his thick muscles and fur (he'd feel nothing like the way Frederick had felt in her arms), but maybe it would help her get in the mood.

Frederick had made spankings sound almost fun.

The Beast was waiting for her, prowling the sunlit atrium where breakfast was served. Bowls of fresh fruit—even oranges, which didn't grow there, and had to have been shipped overseas at quite an expense—beckoned her to the table. Cups of steaming chocolate and little jam-filled pastries made her decision (if it was, indeed, her decision) a bit easier.

She would dine with the Beast, and she would be pleasant, and good Lord in Heaven, she would do whatever she had to

(whatever she desired)

to get herself closer to her release date. To freedom, a mere six months away.

And if she happened to enjoy herself during that six months…well, no one had to know. Here, alone in the castle, only the fairies would be witness to her submission to the Beast's darkest desires.

4

DINING WITH THE BEAST

The Beast caught the girl's scent as she rounded the corner into the atrium. A night in her new suite had done her good—she smelled of rose water and linen, not fear-sweat and hay.

He rose on his hind legs, to help her see him as more human. Still, she gasped and drew back against the doorframe, as if he'd risen to pounce.

"Good morning," he said. "Thank you for joining me."

Belle smiled hesitantly and stepped forward, allowing him to pull her chair out for her. "Thank you, sir."

"If this meal doesn't suit you," he offered, "you can always request something more to your liking."

"This is perfect," she said. "Beast. Sir. Will you sit with me? Please?"

The Beast nodded, his heavy mane swaying down his back. He'd grown unaccustomed to eating properly, at a table, in a chair. With silverware. As the years had worn on, he became more beast than man, and most of his meals now were eaten raw, fresh from hunting in the woods.

"Of course," he said, setting his enormous weight into the chair. "All chairs in this castle should be able to support me," he added, glancing at the chair sternly. He'd given the castle its warning. If the chair broke under him now, it was in big trouble.

"Those fairies of yours are quite something," Belle said, daintily nibbling at a pastry.

"How did you sleep, beauty?" he asked. Had she dreamt what he had dreamt? Did she see him, kiss him, in his human form? Or was last night a memory for him alone?

"Um…" Belle took a sip of chocolate and smiled, as if to apologize for being unable to respond with a full mouth.

The Beast waited. He had nowhere else to be, so Belle was either going to tell him how she slept (if she'd slept at all) or they would have a long, silent meal.

"I had a vivid dream, to be honest. And I awoke feeling less than refreshed."

Belle looked at him closely. What did she see when she stared at him so?

"This castle has a way of doing that," Beast said. "Making dreams seem real."

"I need to know where you're keeping Prince Frederick," she said suddenly.

The Beast's fork clattered from his hand onto the parquet floor. "Pardon?"

"Frederick. I saw him last night. He told me he was here, a prisoner in the castle. I must find him. Please, lead me to him."

"I can't, Belle. That's impossible."

He wanted to. He wished he could scream to the world about what had been done to him, about who he truly was.

"What have I done to upset you?" Belle cried.

The Beast dropped to all fours and paced the wall of windows overlooking the garden. "Nothing, beauty."

"Then please, stop growling at me," she said. "It frightens me."

"If you want to be gone so badly, then perhaps we should get your six month sentence going, don't you think?" he asked. This time, yes, it came out as a growl. Not what he intended, and most definitely not the best way to woo her.

"Yes," she said, standing. "Absolutely. Let's begin and be done with it, once and for all."

The Beast rose once more, until he towered over her. Belle quieted and looked up at him, as if waiting for him to make the first move.

He would, if only he knew what to do, and how to make her love him.

"Very well, he said. "Let's discuss some ground rules."

Belle waited silently.

"You should probably respond with, 'Yes, Sir,'" he offered.

"Yes, Sir," she said.

"We've already decided that I will not harm you, and I will release you in six months—"

"Wonderful," Belle interrupted.

"—provided you do what I say," he finished.

"Yes… Sir. I understand."

"Are you through you with your breakfast, Belle?"

She glanced longingly at an orange. "May I have one of those, first, Sir? I usually only got oranges for Christmas. It's sort of a novelty for me."

The Beast plucked an orange from the bowl of fruit on the table, and snagged the rind with one long fang. She watched with interest as he peeled the fruit for her, revealing the juicy sections inside.

"I want you to become more comfortable with my appearance," he said. "You may eat this from my fingers." He broke off a section and held it out to her.

Belle frowned, but the expression was fleeting. She quickly replaced it with a serene nod. "Of course. I will do whatever you say, as promised."

She took a tentative step toward him, and as she did so, he pulled the orange slightly closer to his body, so that she soon found herself close enough to his body to be in a most intimate range. The Beast offered her the orange slice, and she nibbled it gently from his thick, dark fingers.

"It's delicious, Sir," she said. "But I think I'm quite done now."

"Have another piece," he said, holding out another slice.

"I'm full, thank you."

"That's fine." He set the unfinished orange down on the table and smiled at her.

The poor girl winced, then laughed a bit. "A smile."

"You've pleased me by eating from my hands. But while you may be done eating, I'm not done having you lick at my fingers like a little cat."

Belle's eyes widened.

"Come, put my finger in your mouth. Think of it as an easy way to get used to me."

Belle moaned and looked around the empty atrium, as if seeking an escape.

"You're not ready for this," the Beast said. "We can start your sentence when you're prepared to actually follow instructions."

"No!" she said. "I mean, I am ready. I'm ready." She took his large hand in her two small ones, and ran her fingers along the thick skin and fur that covered the back of his knuckles.

He didn't like seeing her so uncomfortable, but their time together was limited. The sooner she became comfortable with his body, with being near him, touching him, letting him touch her… the better.

Belle pressed her lips to his fingertip and kissed him there.

"Good girl," he said. "Use your tongue."

Her pink tongue darted out past her lips, sliding up his finger for just a moment before she stopped.

"Are you getting some sort of... enjoyment out of this? Is this pleasurable for you?" she asked.

"It's pleasurable for me to see you obeying me, yes. But if you'd rather put your pretty mouth to work on another appendage in order to give me the pleasure you seem to be inquiring about, then go ahead."

Belle gasped and dropped his hand. "I couldn't."

"You don't have to. It's only breakfast time. Perhaps today we'll just touch each other, nothing more. How about that?"

"Yes," she breathed, clearly relieved. "Yes, thank you."

The Beast paused. "Do you...do you *want* to touch me?"

Belle looked up at the Beast, at his massive form. He was so different from anything she'd ever seen before. So beautiful, in a terrifying way. The way a lion is beautiful, even as he stalks his prey.

Yes. She wanted to touch him.

"May I, Sir?"

A low rumble emanated from his chest. "Of course. Go ahead. Don't be afraid, beauty."

Belle touched his abdomen first, perhaps because that was at eye-level, and maybe (most likely) because she loved the tight blocks of muscle, and the fur that covered it seemed so soft.

She ran her fingertips over the brown and black fur, so gently that she didn't even feel the skin beneath it yet. It was soft indeed. She glanced up at him, at those incredible

human, so human

eyes of his, and he smiled. It didn't frighten her, not this time. He appeared to really enjoy her hesitant contact.

With more confidence now, she continued, running her palm across the broad expanse of his chest, finally feeling the firm muscle beneath the fur, muscle that displayed his incredible strength. When she opened both of her arms wide, her fingertips grazed the edges of his forearms. That was how wide he was, how tall he was. His sheer enormity aroused her somehow, made her tingle.

"May I touch your face, Sir?" she asked quietly.

The Beast dropped heavily to all fours, and now his head was even with hers. The lion's mane flowed out from around his face, thick and as vibrant as if it had been spun from gold. His heavy brow felt warm, very warm, or perhaps her hands were chilled.

"That feels nice," he said, as softly as a lover.

Belle stroked his head, bringing her fingers down to his fangs. They were clean and white, and terribly sharp. If she touched the tip of that long canine tooth, would it prick her, would she bleed? She paused, unwilling to get bitten.

"I won't harm you," he repeated. "You have nothing to fear. I have full control over my mouth, my teeth. You could even kiss my lips, and feel nothing but comfort there."

Belle smiled at him, surprised by the Beast's gentleness. It was a bit hard to wrap her head around the idea that he wasn't some wild animal that couldn't be trusted.

Could she really kiss the Beast?

She moved in, her lips hovering close to his. But fear took hold again. "You said today was about touching. Touching alone."

"So be it," he said. Did he sound disappointed?

Before she changed her mind, Belle walked around to the side of the Beast, stroking his silky fur as she went. At some point below his waist, covered now by a pair of custom-tailored pants that only fairies could have provided, his upper torso transformed into that of a wolf-like lower body.

The long, sleek legs, the powerful hind paws, and the tail.

Would he wag his tail if he was pleased? Belle stifled a burst of nervous laughter, and the Beast growled. She felt it vibrate through his massive body.

"Oh!" she gasped, and stepped back.

"You're laughing at me," he said.

He sounded hurt. How could a small laugh from a small girl have hurt the feelings of someone so powerful?

"No, no I wasn't," she said. Belle wasn't even sure if it was a fib or not. Looking at him now, the idea of laughing at such a beast made absolutely no sense.

"What if I had you strip, and I touched every inch of you, and I laughed?" he asked. "What if I laughed at *your* body?" It didn't seem like a threat, rather, it seemed like he really was wounded by her reaction.

"I'm nervous, Beast, Sir, that is all. I had a silly thought and the laugh escaped me. I wouldn't dare laugh at you."

"Strip."

Belle stepped back, her heel bumping up against the doorframe. "Sir, please."

"Remove your clothes, or I will remove them for you."

"Please don't hurt me," she whispered, tears filling her eyes.

"Let's see how you feel, when you are the subject of inspection."

What could she do? She could run, she could tell him no. But he was bigger, and he would win. He was a Beast. There was no reason to make this harder on herself.

"I apologize, Sir," she said. "I truly do."

"Well, then?" he asked, nodding his head toward her gown.

"Perhaps the fairies could provide assistance," she said.

They did. Her gown dropped to her feet like a puddle, the secret diary she'd stored in the folds hitting the marble floor with a thud, but the Beast didn't appear to notice. With renewed courage, she stepped out of the fabric, naked. Naked in the sunlight, exposed completely to her Beast, her Master.

The Beast circled her like a wolf circling its prey. Belle closed her eyes, taking calming breaths. He wouldn't harm her, he had promised. If he wished to, he could. So there was nothing to do but leave her fate up to Providence.

"You can laugh at me if you must, Beast," she whispered. "I know you want to."

"No, Beauty. There is nothing I see to laugh at. You are beautiful, and fully deserving of your name."

Belle opened her eyes. He was so close, mere millimeters away.

"Touch me?" she asked.

Why did he arouse her so? The memory of what he'd done to her on her first night in the cell, when she'd parted her thighs for him and welcomed his touch on her wet heat—despite her fear—came back to her so hard she moaned.

"You *want* me to touch you?" he asked, as if in disbelief. "You're not afraid?"

"I'm not afraid, Sir."

Touch me. Touch me there, once more.

He reached out and picked her up, cradling her in his arms like a babe. Even though she was now quite high off the marble floor, she had no fear of falling, or of him dropping her. She felt…safe.

Safe in the arms of the Beast.

The Beast trailed his fingers across her cheek, his touch so sweet and gentle, she sighed with pleasure.

"What were you laughing at, little one?" he asked. "Tell me."

Heat filled her cheeks, warming them. "I am so sorry, Sir."

His hand dropped to her naked breast, her nipple hard as ice—whether from arousal or fear, or both, she wasn't certain.

"I wondered if you ever wagged your tail to display happiness," she mumbled. She winced, pressing her face against his warm, fuzzy chest.

But he laughed!

"Wh-what?" she asked. "Are you angry?"

"I don't wag my tail, no. I suppose it's because—" he broke off in lilting growls, growls that made no sense.

"Please don't growl at me, Sir," she said desperately. Now she felt vulnerable, the way she should have felt all along, perhaps, naked and carried in his arms.

"I don't mean to growl," he said. His voice changed, now he sounded very serious. "One of my—afflictions—is that I can't always communicate the way I would like to. Sometimes I am more Beast than man. But with you, Beauty, I want to be as much of man as you'll allow."

"Are you—are you a man, Beast?"

He looked at her with those intense green eyes. "I'll let you decide, in time."

"Beast?" she whispered.

"Beauty."

"That thing you did that first night I was here—"

"I'm so sorry, Belle. I took advantage of you. You must have been horribly frightened." He brought his face close to hers, almost as if to comfort her, to cuddle her. "I forgive you for wounding me with that wicked saw. I suppose I'm lucky you didn't ask the ah, fairies for an ax to chop off my head."

"Yes, I was frightened," she admitted. "But that's because I thought you might eat me. I'm afraid of dying, Beast, not of having a pleasurable experience." Belle blushed.

The Beast grinned. "I'm glad we're on the same page, then."

"Will you do that thing again?" she asked. "Will you touch me the way you did that night?"

"Ah, Belle," he said. "I could, but first you must earn it. From now on, you shall earn your pleasure." The Beast set her down on her feet. "Let's go to the parlor, where we can be more comfortable."

Belle followed him, naked. It felt so strange to walk freely through the castle without clothing, but since no one but the fairies could see them, she supposed it didn't matter much.

What did he mean, she'd have to earn it?

Would he spank her again, as Frederick seemed to imply in her dream

(was it a dream?)

last night? And where was Frederick, if not only in her dreams? Would the Beast tell her where he had imprisoned the handsome prince?

5

BELLE'S PUNISHMENT

The Beast took her into the parlor and stood before the fireplace. "Fire," he commanded, and flames burst to life behind him, crackling.

"What do you want me to do, Sir?"

She was nervous, yes, but after her unusual evening with Frederick, she had to admit she was intrigued. Why had Frederick told her that she must love the Beast? Belle would never be able to love the monster who held her captive, who kept her from her Papa. The monster who knew exactly what to do to make her writhe with pleasure...

"Come, sit on my lap," he said, his words thick with desire. "To earn your reward, you only have to ask me two questions, and answer one."

Belle walked over to him and sat on his large lap, the fine wool of his trousers soft beneath her flesh. For some reason she wished that she could feel his fur on her bottom, on her thighs. What did the Beast's most private parts look like?

"If I may be so bold," she said, "why do you want me to ask you questions?"

"I want you to get to know me, and I want to get to know you." He didn't smile, but his reason seemed friendly enough.

"I'm scared to say the wrong thing. I don't want you to spank me again." Belle blushed as she spoke, but mainly because she wasn't quite sure that wasn't a lie.

When Frederick had told her that the Beast enjoyed spanking her, and that Frederick would spank her and make her love it, she believed him. Maybe she could love it, or some aspect of it. Maybe she didn't have to feel hurt or humiliated by a spanking in an adult setting. After all, she was no longer a child.

"I will never harm you," the Beast said. "You don't need to be afraid that I'll spank you, because I *will* spank you. As long as you know for a fact that I will, there is no need to fear it."

Belle inhaled sharply. That made a twisted sort of sense. It wasn't a question of if, it was a question of when. Still, her stomach tumbled at the thought.

The Beast positioned her on his lap so that they could look at each other quite comfortably. He was very close, close enough to feel the heat of his breath as it passed his sharp, shiny fangs.

"What would you like to know about me, Belle?"

"Why did you take me captive?" she asked immediately.

"Because you offered yourself in lieu of your father. I'd rather have a beautiful young woman than an old man in my dungeon, anyway."

Belle frowned. "Why not just let my Papa go? Why did you force me to take his place to begin with?"

"I couldn't let your Papa go, Belle," the Beast said. "Not when I discovered he had a daughter. You."

"Why not let me go?" she whispered.

"You've asked your questions," he said. "You can save the others for another interview, another time."

The Beast ran his hand down to her thighs, gently spreading

them, until her cunny was accessible to his slow, careful tactile inspection. "Now, Beauty, I have a question for *you*."

Belle moaned as he slid one thick finger along her nether lips, spreading them until her tender bud was exposed. She was already wet with need.

"All right," she breathed.

"What do you know about Frederick?"

"It was just a dream," Belle said. The Beast touched her clitoris, rubbed it so gently that she arched her back, trying to get more contact with his fingers. "At least, I think it was a dream."

"Go on," he said. Without pause, he tickled her wetness, spreading her labia and teasing her tender bud.

"He told me to love you. And he told me he was... he is imprisoned here. I know he's here, somewhere, Beast. Won't you tell me where he is?"

"Do you like Frederick? Did you do anything naughty with him that you need to tell me about?"

Belle moaned as the Beast rubbed her clit faster. "No! At least, I don't think so. Maybe."

"It's all right, Belle," he said. "You can play with your dream companion. As long as you don't forget that you serve me, above all."

"I won't forget, Sir. Please, please," she broke off as he slid one thick finger deep inside her, making her gasp in pleasure.

Oh Lord in Heaven, the Beast had a way with his hands!

The Beast hit a spot inside her, something that felt like it would make her melt into a puddle. But, it also made her a bit uncomfortable.

"Beast, please, I have to..."

Oh no, she had to relieve herself. The pressure his huge fingers inside of her, pressing, tapping over and over against that spot, made her feel like she could barely hold it in. At least (in her admittedly limited experience) that was what it felt like.

"I don't care," he said. "Relax into the feeling, Beauty."

"Stop!" she begged. "I might have an accident, please, stop."

"I don't care," he said. "Go ahead."

But she couldn't, she wouldn't. As if against her will (although she very much enjoyed the feeling, if only she didn't have to pee) the Beast tore a slow, shuddering orgasm from her. Warm wetness gushed from her vagina.

"Oh no," she cried, hiding her face against his chest. "I'm so sorry."

The Beast laughed. "You didn't have an accident, Beauty. You had an orgasm."

No, that made no sense. She'd had an orgasm before with him, and this was different. She could feel the wetness.

"It's your arousal, nothing sinister. Sometimes, if a woman is stimulated in just the right way, she can ejaculate." The Beast lifted his wet hand to her face for inspection. "Lick it," he said.

Belle grimaced. "Please don't make me, Sir."

"Lick my finger, because it will please me. And then you'll see you have nothing to be embarrassed about."

She leaned forward and sniffed his hand. No, it didn't smell like urine. Had she really ejaculated, like a man? How odd! But the Beast seemed to be happy about it, as if she'd done something he approved of. With a quick dart of her tongue, she licked her own fluids from his hand.

"Good girl," he said.

His praise helped dissipate the lingering embarrassment, and tasting her own wetness had, surprisingly, aroused her more than she would ever have imagined. Still, it felt so strange, so dangerous and wrong, to do such things with the Beast.

"Beast," she whispered. "Where is Frederick?"

She was scared, scared that the Beast would be angry with her for asking again about the handsome prince. Surely he must hate that another man, one who she was attracted to and who might take her attention from him, was here in the castle.

But he had told her she was free to "play" with him.

The Beast, if nothing else, had a way of surprising her.

The Beast looked at Belle's sweet, frightened expression. "Darling, I can't tell you. But you need not fear Frederick, just as you need not fear me."

He couldn't tell her that he knew of her dream. That he had, somehow, been a part of her dream. It didn't seem possible, and yet it had happened.

They both had fallen asleep, and met again in another realm, perhaps. It had never happened to him before.

Well, that wasn't exactly so. In his dreams, all alone for the past decade in the castle, he was always a man. In his dreams, the Beast was Frederick. He'd always assumed that his dreams were fantasy alone, a misty false memory created in sleep.

Not actually occurring. And yet, they must have been real, or how would he know, down to the last detail, exactly why Belle kept asking about Frederick? The Beast hadn't asked her for specifics of her encounter with his most inner self, but he knew.

He *knew*.

It would be beneficial for her to love him as Frederick, but only because if he ever did turn back into his former state, she would know him. As it stood, if she thought Frederick was someone else, and loved him, then how (or why) would she ever pick a Beast to love?

There had to be a way for the Beast to convince her to be with him, through Frederick. Her dream had already convinced her to start her training with the Beast, to start to get to know him. But she kept harping on finding Frederick in waking life.

That would have to stop.

"Belle, I know you're concerned about Frederick."

"I saw him, I think, I don't know…" she whispered.

"But if you mention him to me again, if you continue to search the castle for him, then you will be punished."

"That's not fair," she said, pushing off of his lap. "He came to me, he's held prisoner here."

"Belle, you need to stop," he warned.

"And you said that you didn't mind if I was with him! Why change your mind now?"

"You can be with him, if he comes to you," the Beast agreed. "But stop searching for him. Forget about him, when you are with me."

Belle turned her face from the Beast and stormed, naked, back toward the hallway.

"When you are ready to continue, Belle, you will meet me in the dungeon."

Now, she turned on her feet, and glared at him. "I don't understand you, Beast. You are an enigma."

"I am your Master for the next six months," he said softly, his words rumbling as the animalist part of him shone through. "I gave you a direct order, which you immediately disobeyed."

Her eyes widened. Ahh, now she understood.

But she ran away.

The Beast waited for a few minutes for her to realize the error of her ways and return, but she didn't. He could easily grab her and physically take her downstairs for her punishment, but that would be completely in contrast to the point he hoped to make.

She needed to choose this. So, he would wait until she was ready.

It was nightfall before he heard the sound of her suite door squeak open. The Beast paused in his tracks, listening.

Belle stood before him in her dressing gown, looking at her feet sorrowfully.

"Please don't punish me, Sir," she said. She dropped to her knees on the cold stone floor in an unexpected display of submission. "I wasn't thinking."

"You were thinking quite clearly," he said. "You thought you would test me. That's fine. I enjoy punishing misbehaving young women. If you're ready to continue, we shall do so in the dungeon."

She hesitated, her eyes wet with unshed tears of terror. Why should she be so frightened? He had already promised he would never harm her, or eat her.

"I don't want to go to the dungeon," she said.

The Beast raised his brow, giving her a stern look, and she flew down the stairs to the dungeon, suddenly ready to obey.

Good.

Belle stumbled down the long, narrow stairway to the dungeon. Why, why had she pushed so hard? They had been having such a nice time, and she had ruined it all. It helped, a little, to know that the Beast had promised to not ever eat her, and she believed him. Perhaps that was why she finally worked up the courage to face him again. Only took her all day.

Still, he'd also promised to punish her. Would he spank her again, right now? Or would it be something else, something that required a dungeon, and not just her, overturned on his lap?

The Beast was right behind her. She felt cornered, and she once again dropped to her knees, hoping it would appease him.

"I like that, Belle," he said, the earlier anger from that morning gone from his voice.

"I want to please you, Sir," she said. "I know I promised to do what you say. I'm trying, I am."

"You may stand," he said. "Take off your dress."

He prowled over to a set of chains hanging on the dungeon's cold, stone wall. How had she not noticed those before?

Belle swallowed hard and rushed to obey. She wouldn't tarry

and give him more reason to be hard on her. She'd learned her lesson about stalling after her first spanking.

The chains moved as if on their accord, latching thick cuffs around her wrists.

Oh fairies, are you against me too, now?

The Beast stepped back, his gaze on her naked, stretched body, her arms high above her head, and smiled, baring his sharp teeth.

"Have you ever been whipped, Beauty?" he asked.

What was the right answer? If she said yes (a lie), would he go easier on her, or harder?

"No, Beast," she whispered.

"Would you like to be whipped?"

A trick question. It had to be.

"I'm scared, Sir," she said honestly. "But I'll do whatever you want me to do. We have an agreement, and I know if I do what you say, then you'll honor your end of the bargain and set me free when it is time."

The Beast laughed, a low, rumbling sound, and she struggled to keep her face expressionless despite her concern. He would honor their deal, right? He had to.

"That's right, Belle. We will both keep our word." He left her field of vision, disappearing into the shadows, and returned with a long, leather whip with several strands of leather hanging ominously from his hand.

"This will hurt, but the marks won't last more than tonight, and by tomorrow morning, your skin will be as white and unblemished as it is right now. I chose this whip because it hurts, but doesn't harm. I keep my word, always, Beauty."

A whimper escaped her throat, and she swallowed again, determined to not cry. She could handle this. How much could it hurt if it didn't even leave a lasting mark, right?

He dropped to all fours and moved in closer, nudging her torso with his head, the long, silky mane brushing against her nipples. The tiny pink peaks were hard, and while Belle wished she could say it was only because she was freezing, in reality, she was aroused.

Why? Why, why, and how on earth was she turned on when she was about to be punished by the Beast?

"Turn around," he said.

She obeyed, the chains around her wrists rattling in protest as her nipples pressed against the stone. The wall felt icy, almost wet.

"You will count," he said.

"How many, Sir?" *Please, please don't be a lot.*

"I will stop when I feel you've had enough. I have considered one lash for every hour you kept me waiting…" He paused. "Perhaps next time you won't give me all day to think about it."

With that, he stood on his hind legs, and once again she felt so small next to his towering mass. The helplessness of her situation overwhelmed her. Chained to his dungeon wall, unable to break free, unable to leave, forced to accept whatever punishment he deemed fit to give her.

For some reason, that very helplessness soothed her, and made it all right. If she couldn't escape, then she may as well relax, and not fight. He could do what he wanted, and she would survive, because he promised her so.

And she believed him. The Beast, in everything he had done and said, had always been honest with her. She was safe in his care.

The whip made a horrible whistling sound as it swooshed through the cold air and lashed across her back. Belle shrieked, more in surprise than pain—although the pain was there, definitely— a sharp burn across her tender flesh.

"Count them off, Belle," he ordered.

"One," she said, surprised her voice was so strong. It filled the dungeon.

He took the whip and turned it around in his hand, so that the thick handle faced her. No! He couldn't beat her with the handle, she would break into pieces.

"Please," she whispered, but the Beast shook his head.

"You forgot to say Sir," he said.

She winced, waiting for the force of the thick handle of the whip, but it didn't come. Instead, he nudged the handle between her legs, rubbing it against her clit slowly.

What on earth? She closed her eyes, resting her forehead against the dungeon wall, as he slid the handle, not inside her, no, but back and forth along her clit.

She gasped as pleasure flowed over her, but then, he stopped. No!

"Please," she said again, but this time she had no idea what she pleaded for. For more? Yes. More.

But the lash whistled through the air again, striking her on the buttocks this time. Belle cried out.

"Two, Sir," she said, her body twisting in the chains.

Another lash of the whip. Oh God, the agony!

"Three, Sir," she cried.

And then, the handle of the whip was between her shaking thighs once more. She bucked her hips against it, grinding her cunny down onto the handle, needing more. The Beast teased her, bringing her once more to the brink of climax before stopping completely.

She cried out again, before he even whipped her, when he stopped. Now she craved that lash, because if she could just live through that moment of pain, he would reward her.

Unless this—this teasing—was also her punishment. A sob wracked through her as the lash flicked against her thighs.

"Four, Sir," she said. Again.

"Five, Sir. Six, Sir. Oh God, please, Beast, please—"

Now his hands were on her, running along the flare of her

hips, and finally settling between her thighs. Moisture ran down her inner thighs, and she hid her face in the crook of her elbow. It felt so good, too good.

"Please," she begged, and he kept rubbing her there, so slowly, so tortuously.

"Please, what?" he asked, and took her long hair in one meaty fist, forcing her to unhide her face.

"Please, Sir, Beast. Please let me come."

"You are being punished, Beauty," he said softly. He played with her clit again, moving his thick fingers so slowly she thought she might die.

And then he stopped. The Beast unchained her, and she sighed with gratitude, but her relief was short lived. He immediately repositioned her arms behind her and latched her wrists to the stone wall once more.

While the new position made her more comfortable than she'd been with her arms so high above her head, being bound in the Beast's dungeon left her little room to be grateful for that small kindness.

"You'll stay here tonight," he said. "It will make you appreciate your accommodations in your suite upstairs, and our...arrangement."

"Don't leave me like this, Beast," she begged, stepping forward the small bit her restraints would allow. The chains clattered as they bounced against the stone.

"*You* left *me*, Belle. You're the one who walked away first."

She groaned miserably, and his expression softened, as if he couldn't help but to feel sorry for her.

"Perhaps in your dreams," he said, "your playmate will relieve your discomfort."

The Beast withdrew, leaving her alone once more in the cold, dark dungeon.

SHOSHANNA EVERS

6

BEAUTY'S LIBRARY

The Beast wanted to see her in her dreams, he did. He wanted to be Frederick with her once more.

He took a glass of whiskey to the parlor and sat heavily. Could he sleep when she did—and was that even a requisite for the magic to work? The poor girl, how would she sleep when he'd left her in such an uncomfortable state?

The Beast went over to his desk and picked up the looking glass. The looking glass was no ordinary mirror; like most items in his castle, it had not escaped the enchantress's spell. This particular mirror could show him anything he wished to see, without having to leave the castle walls.

"Show me my Beauty," he said, staring at his monstrous reflection.

A swirl of fog hazed the looking glass, then cleared as if by a sudden breeze. Belle was as he'd left her, naked, chained to the dungeon wall, and in the sweetest distress he'd ever seen. She turned in her restraints, rolling her head back against the wall, and sighed.

"Sleep, Belle. I'll see you soon." The Beast set the looking glass down, knowing she couldn't hear him, and sipped deeply from his glass of whiskey.

The wound on his chest was feeling better, so he didn't have much of an excuse for laudanam, but perhaps he should take some anyway? Something, something to send him off to dreamland, where he could regain his masculine form and comfort his beautiful prisoner.

But the events of the day settled on his shoulders, and as he sat, he drifted off on his own, the glass dropping from his hand harmlessly to the sofa, only narrowly missing the stone floor by centimeters.

And in his sleep, he was Frederick.

Frederick rose from the sofa and ran his hands over his torso, confirming that he was, indeed, himself. He grinned rakishly and bounded down the hall to the dungeon stairs. What time was it? Would Beauty be ready for him?

"Belle?" he whispered into the darkness of the dungeon.

"H-hello?" she replied, from the far wall. "I'm here!"

Frederick lit a sconce on the wall, and warm light flooded their corner of the dungeon. Belle hid her face, as if doing so would somehow make her less naked, less vulnerable.

"Are you all right?" Frederick asked. "What have you done to be punished like this?"

He knew it had to do with the Beast, but at the moment, the two worlds seemed so far apart. Which was his true self, the Beast or the Prince? He didn't know, himself. Right now, he was Frederick. That was all that mattered.

"I'm fine," Belle said, finally peeking out from behind her curtain of hair. "The Beast had a lesson to teach me, and I do, I suppose, have quite a bit to learn." She laughed, an unexpected sound, considering her predicament.

He smiled. "You're in quite the good spirits, considering you are naked and chained to a wall, and I am a man known for my love of bound women."

At this, she smiled. "It's only a dream, you can do anything to me in a dream. Nothing matters if it's not real."

He stepped closer, close enough to feel the heat radiating off of her naked flesh. "What if it is real?"

"Then I truly am in a predicament." Belle laughed nervously. "Am I safe with you, Frederick?"

Her lips were so full, begging for a kiss. He smoothed her hair out of her face and smiled. "I won't harm you."

"You sound like my Beast."

"Mmmm." Frederick leaned in and kissed her lips gently, then pulled back, waiting for her response.

"It is a dream, right?"

"I don't know," he replied honestly. Was it? "I think so."

"I've been searching for you. The Beast won't tell me where he's keeping you captive in the castle. How did you find me?"

Frederick frowned. "I knew where you were. Perhaps the castle guided me to you." He shrugged. "Does it matter? I'm here. I've missed you."

Belle smiled. "I missed you too. I did as you told me, Frederick. I agreed to begin my service to the Beast."

"Good!" Joy filled him, but he wasn't sure why. Yes, it was good. She needed to be with the Beast. To fall in love with the Beast.

"Why?" she whispered, echoing the very same question floating through his own mind. "Why would you want me to be with anyone other than you?"

"It's not because I care for you any less, Beauty. I can't explain it. Just know that the Beast is good, and he adores you. You must learn to love the Beast."

"He left me in quite the state," she mumbled. "Will you rescue me? Or are you here to take advantage of a captive woman?"

"Both," he grinned, his mouth close to hers. "Let's do both."

"All right," she giggled.

Belle stood on her tiptoes, pressing her mouth to his, her eyes shining brightly with excitement.

"Let me see if I can rescue you from this particular predicament you're in," he suggested, dropping his hand down to the curve of her waist. "Open your thighs for me."

She breathed out shakily, and obeyed. Before he could even bring his fingers to her wet heat, Belle moaned in anticipation.

"You've really been left wanting, now haven't you?" he asked, touching her clit.

"Yes," she said, pushing her hips forward, as if hoping to pull his fingers into her body by sheer force of will.

He opened her nether lips, teasing the edges of her tiny bud.

"Oh, Frederick, yes…"

"This is a fine look on you," he murmured.

"Please, please."

Frederick gave her a warning swat on her bottom and she jumped, the chains rattling. When she stilled, her resumed his ministrations. One finger inside her, then two… rubbing his hand against her cunny until she ground against him, crying out in pleasure.

"Do you like this?" he asked, although the wetness covering his hand told her tale.

"I do, Frederick, I do."

Then, like the Beast had done before, he stopped, leaving her on the brink of climax. She nearly screamed in frustration at another thwarted orgasm.

Now he had her full attention. "You must learn to love the Beast, Belle. Can you do that for me?"

Her eyes were clear but wild with lust as she stared at him. "I will do anything for you, Frederick. Anything."

Satisfied, he built up a steady rhythm, faster and faster, until Belle cried out, the chains clattering against the stone and her screams of passion echoing throughout the underground lair.

When she was finished, she rested her head against her arm once more, panting.

"Do you have a key?" she asked, after a few moments.

Frederick laughed. "A key, that's what you want me for? I feel used."

"I want you for all sorts of things," she said. "But a key would be especially useful at this juncture."

"I have a key for your juncture," he teased, reaching for his belt buckle.

"No!" she gasped. "You mustn't! The Beast knows I'm a virgin. If you take me, he'll know."

"Don't you want me?"

"Do I have any choice in the matter?" she asked. Her voice had lost its desirous ring. Now she sounded sad.

He had still only been teasing, and not in the least put off her refusal. But her response wounded him.

Quickly, Frederick pulled the keys off of the far wall and unlatched her restraints, careful to support her as he set her free. She sank to the floor and pulled her knees to her chest.

"Thank you," she said.

"You have a choice, Belle," he said. "With me, with the Beast, you can choose. It may not feel like it, but I care for your happiness. I know the Beast does too."

"How do you know what the Beast cares for?"

"He could've ravished you the moment he had you to himself. There was no need to give you a suite, or time to decide how you felt about things, or any of that. You are his prisoner, Belle. You belong to him until he sets you free. Don't you see that?"

"Oh yes, I see that quite clearly."

"And yet, you still remain a virgin."

A look of understanding crossed her face. "I suppose. But he will take me eventually."

Frederick smiled at her and sat down on the cold stone floor beside her. "And when he does, it will be wonderful. You'll want it as badly as you wanted me to touch you just now."

"When I'm with you," she said, "that doesn't seem possible. But when…when I'm alone with the Beast, something comes over me. A strange desire, mixed right in with my fear. Is that odd?"

"Not very, no."

"Why don't you escape, Frederick?"

He laughed. "And miss out on getting to know the most beautiful girl I've ever seen? No thank you." He stretched his legs out in front of him and wrapped an arm around her slender shoulders. "I'll stay right here, if it's all right with you."

She was quiet for a moment. "Yes. It's all right with me."

Dawn broke, and with it, Belle discovered she had been broken too. Not broken in a bad way, really. Just…bent. She'd been emotionally bent, her will twisted until she no longer knew what she wanted, what Frederick wanted of her, or what the Beast wanted from her.

What did *she* want?

(I want to see my Papa)

But that thought, so ever-present and insistent before, seemed submerged now just below the surface.

More pressing issues were at hand. A new world of possibilities had been opened for her, and she wanted to explore them more fully before she went back home. Life with Papa was simple bliss, the warmth of hearth and home, but life in the castle with an intimidating and magnetic Beast and magical fairies and a prince who may or may not be a figment of her imagination…well, it was all a bit too intriguing to give up so quickly.

Especially since she'd come to the castle with no concept of her own womanhood, her own natural ability for pleasure. She had so much to learn, and the Beast had her as his captive student to teach—by any means necessary—exactly what she was capable of.

Today, instead of dreading her training under the Beast's stern hand, she was almost excited.

Have I gone mad? Delusions, hallucinations?

Perhaps she was locked up with the lunatics herself, humping the walls and moaning for relief whenever an attendant walked by. Perhaps she hadn't spent the night chained to a dungeon wall, but in a straightjacket. That would almost make more sense than her new, strange reality.

Frederick was nowhere to be found. At some point he'd chained her back to the wall, although the other possibility—that he'd never been there at all, and she'd merely dreamt the entire experience—was also a distinct possibility.

How could she make informed decisions when she had no concept of what was even real anymore?

"Beast," she whispered to the empty dungeon.

His heavy paws sounded on the long stairway. There was no way he could have heard her speak, she'd barely breathed the word aloud at all. And yet, he arrived before her as if summoned.

"Good morning, Belle," the Beast said. He nodded his head toward her shackles, and they released.

"Thank you, Sir," she said.

"Come to me."

Fear thrummed through her body, but she fought past it and stepped forward to him. What would he do to her?

But the Beast tenderly took her small wrists in his large hands, rubbing away the soreness, and inspecting her skin closely. He turned her around, running his hands along her back and down to her buttocks and thighs. His very touch ignited that same fiery passion she couldn't deny, even though it conflicted so completely with her fear of him.

"Just as I promised, Beauty," he said. "You are unmarked from my lash."

"You are a man of your word, Sir," she whispered.

"A man," he murmured, almost under his breath.

She couldn't tell if she'd offended him or not. He was, by his own admission, not any man. He was *The Beast*. The very Beast who had frightened her so terribly that she'd inflicted physical damage upon him, leaving a red, healing wound on his chest, right across his heart.

But—

"What's wrong, my darling?" the Beast asked.

She loved that he could sense her emotions shifting, the questions building inside of her, without her having to say a word. Even her own family couldn't do that with her.

"I had the oddest thought," she said. "I can't say, it's too embarrassing."

Now the Beast smiled, showcasing his impressive fangs. "Let's trade confessions, then. We'll be even, and you won't feel embarrassed about whatever you were thinking anymore."

Belle smiled brightly at the idea. Even the fact that the Beast seemed so intent on getting to know the true woman she was, beyond her face and body—well, it meant a lot. Most of her suitors only cared to court her for her dowry, back when she was rich. After her Papa lost everything, the men who came knocking only cared about her appearance. They wanted to see if she lived up to her given name.

No one, save the Beast, had ever offered to share confessions before. Or required that they learn more about each other before he rewarded her with an orgasm. No one had ever given her an orgasm before, period.

What sort of Beast was this man?

What sort of man was a Beast?

"I want to be marked by you, Sir," she admitted. "I'm afraid of the pain, but...I think it will help me know what's real. Almost like how you pinch yourself to be sure you're not dreaming... If I could see the marks on my body then I'd know I wasn't going insane. That I'm truly here, with you."

The Beast smiled, but she was growing accustomed to his fangs, and didn't flinch.

"That's my confession," she added. "May I hear yours?"

"I confess that I know you're unhappy about being held captive here in my castle, with me. And while—for reasons I can't divulge—I can't grant you your freedom early, what I can do is make your stay more enjoyable. I would like to do something that will make you happy...as long as you don't request your freedom."

Belle threw her arms around his thick, muscular waist in a moment of pure excitement, then quickly withdrew, unsure if such displays of affection were appropriate.

"Thank you, Beast. That's so very kind."

"And I haven't forgotten what you've confessed to me, either," he added. "I'd be more than delighted to honor your request to be marked."

Butterflies flitted through her belly at the thought, but she just smiled. There was no need to fear, because the Beast would keep her safe—even from himself.

"The lady needs a gown," he said to some spot on the ceiling. Could he see the fairies?

Before she could wonder more about it, she found herself dressed in a shimmering blue gown with chiffon and lace. Tiny satin slippers appeared on her feet.

"Thank you, Sir," she said, touching the material in awe. The stitching was so fine, it was nearly unnoticeable. "It's beautiful."

"Then it suits you," he said. "Come, let's leave the dungeon and your punishment behind for the day. Tell me what you desire, and I'll give you whatever you wish."

As long as I don't wish to leave…

But she tamped down the thought and smiled up at her captor brightly.

"I love to read. If you have any books lying about, I'd be most grateful for an opportunity to read them. It will help the hours go by when we're not, um…together."

She whispered the last word, since being *together* with him was not as simple as that. Being with the Beast meant lessons in humility, passion, and pain. Belle could never be bored when the Beast was near.

They climbed the steep staircase out of the dungeon, and Belle gasped in delight at the sight of the great room. It was filled with roses, everywhere. The scarlet blooms filled the hall with their glorious scent, and with the sunlight streaming through the stained-glass windows, the interior of the castle was transformed into a magical paradise.

"It's beautiful," she breathed.

"Then it suits you, as well," he said, smiling down at her. "I never cut roses before you arrived. I was afraid to kill them before their time. But now, it seems that the roses truly come alive only when they are in your presence."

Belle blushed at the heady praise, and lowered her eyes.

"Come with me," he said, taking her hand in his. His hand seemed to swallow hers whole. "Allow me to show you the library."

"You have a library?" She bounced a bit on the balls of her feet in excitement, but stopped herself. She wanted to behave like a lady, not a schoolgirl.

The Beast led her down the long corridor to the West wing, and pushed open a large, imposing mahogany door.

"Close your eyes," the Beast said playfully, and pulled her by the hand into the library.

Belle obeyed, but she couldn't help but to breath in the scent of books—that incredible aroma of old paper, glue, ink, and leather, combined with a hint of the magic that made the words come alive on the page.

"You can open your eyes now."

Belle blinked at the vision before her and inhaled sharply. Books! Books *everywhere*. The enormous room was two stories tall, with a spiraling stairway on each side leading up to the upper level. Leather-bound volumes filled the shelves from floor to ceiling on both floors, and the upper level looked down upon them with an open loft area surrounded by an ornate wrought-iron railing.

Several rolling ladders were in front of the bookcases to allow easy access to even the highest-placed books. And best of all were the chairs and couches around the floor, and the pillows piled high by the windows, perfect for getting comfortable with a story. The library was filled with sunlight during the day, as well as having numerous lamps available for cozy nighttime reading.

"Does it please you?" the Beast asked.

He sounded worried, and Belle realized she hadn't said a word since he brought her inside. She'd simply been standing there, looking around with her mouth hanging open.

"I've always wished that this might be what the Kingdom of Heaven looks like," she said. "It's amazing. It's…it's perfect. Thank you, Beast."

"You're welcome," he said. "I hope it can be some comfort to you during your time here."

"Can I look around a bit?" She picked one thick volume off the nearest shelf and ran her hands lovingly over the binding.

"Certainly," the Beast said. "I have other things to attend to. But I'll see you this afternoon, at which point I will mark you."

Belle was so entranced with the idea of having hours of leisure time to spend perusing the library that she almost didn't catch what he said.

Her reply caught in her throat, and she coughed fitfully. "Sorry, Sir," she said, finally taking in a full breath. "What had seemed like a good idea in the middle of the night when I was chained to your dungeon wall, unsure if I was going insane or not...no longer seems like such a good idea after all."

The Beast shook his head as he walked toward the exit. "You were right, Belle. You need a physical reminder, something you can look at and be reminded of why I am keeping you here."

"Why *are* you keeping me?" she asked immediately.

But he only growled in response. She winced and turned away.

His heavy hand on her shoulder gave her a start, and he sighed. "I'm sorry, Beauty. Sometimes I can't say what needs to be said. But later, perhaps I can show you."

Belle's grip tightened on the book in her hand.

What would the Beast do to mark her?

And most pressing of all, why, oh why, had she asked for this?

7

MARKED BY THE BEAST

Belle watched silently as the Beast left the library, closing the heavy mahogany door behind him.

Part of her wanted to find a good book and lose herself in the story, to mentally leave this place behind as she soared through an adventure of written words. But the more rational—albeit frightened—part of her wanted to know what she could expect to happen that afternoon when the Beast summoned her once more.

If only Frederick were there with her, perhaps he could suggest what the Beast might do to mark her. After all, both Frederick and the Beast seemed to share the same sexual proclivities.

Frederick only seemed to appear when she was dreaming, however, and there was no way she could take a nap right now, not when her nerves were frayed with worry.

She set the book in her hand back onto the bookshelf near her, and remembered. The diary! If she could read Frederick's diary, perhaps she could find a story in which he had marked one of his mistresses, or fantasized about it.

"I wish for Frederick's diary, fairies, if you please."

The old diary appeared, opened to the last page she'd read, laying on an overstuffed cushion by the windowsill.

Belle rushed over to it and sat, her gown settling around her like a shimmery blue pool, and picked up the forbidden diary.

~~~

For my seventeenth birthday, the King is holding a grand ball. It's less a celebration for me, than a chance to please his Queen. My Stepmother loves to show off in front of the court like a peacock.

All was not wasted, however. The seamstress who came in to design Stepmother's gown has taken a liking to me, and didn't blink an eye when I suggested she allow me to stripe her thighs for my birthday. The cane that marked her pale thighs felt so right in my hands, and fit me better than a crown ever could.

The seamstress remarked that she's never met a man of my young age who can make her feel the way that I did. Flattery, no doubt, but it made me feel better than anything a lover has ever said to me.

I suppose I don't really belong here. I write this now, my diary hidden under the table, as everyone dances around the ballroom pretending to celebrate my birthday. No one even glances my way.

I would give up all my riches to find a lover who can truly see me.

~~~

Poor, poor young Prince Frederick! Belle clasped the diary to her chest, momentarily forgetting she was searching for ways in which men might want to mark a woman.

The Frederick she knew from her dreams

(if they were really dreams)

was older, wiser, but still seemed to maintain that sense of self-awareness. The diary entry was written eleven years ago, making Frederick twenty-eight now. Quite a bit older than her nineteen years, but that didn't bother her. If he remained imprisoned in the castle all this time, how could he ever find a lover who could "truly see" him?

No wonder he seemed desperate to connect with her. She wanted to be with him, too. Everything about Frederick turned her on—his handsome face, his dashing smile, those broad, athletic shoulders...

Belle sighed happily. Perhaps tonight she would see him again. They almost had intimate relations last night—they would have, indeed, if she had allowed him. The mere fact that she was chained to a wall naked before him, and still he respected her and listened when she denied him, was testament to his moral character.

She could see herself falling in love with Frederick. But how? How does one fall in love with a man who very likely only exists in her own imagination?

And still, there was the issue that Frederick insisted she learn to love the Beast. The thought was not as horrifying as it had been when she first met the Beast. He was not unlovable, nor terrible, as she had previously thought.

The Beast was not a monster. In appearance, perhaps, but...no. Even his appearance was beginning to grow on her. All those muscles, that strong body, his beautiful *(human)* green eyes. Only Frederick had green eyes as amazing as the Beast. No one else she'd ever met in her short time on Earth had eyes like those.

Eyes that could see into her soul.

Belle set the diary down, and raised her eyebrow. Aha! Perhaps the Beast wanted to stripe her thighs with a cane, the way Frederick had done to his seamstress lover.

A caning. It would hurt, no doubt. But she could handle it. And then she'd be marked, and she could look at her skin and know that this was real. That she wasn't insane, locked up and under Mrs. Sharone's care.

With that thought squared away, Belle was able to set the diary aside and begin exploring the many books the library had to offer. She may as well sit comfortably while she could.

The Beast ran through the woods, the wind rushing through his mane, his paws pounding against the packed dirt on the forest floor. The trees overhead shaded his massive body, and, as only the woods were able to, made him feel *free*.

Presenting the library to Belle had been a gratifying experience. He'd have to have a plaque placed on the door naming the library in her honor. The library had never had a name before, but now it only felt fitting that it should belong to her, as mistress of the castle.

Would she, could she, ever desire to stay with him?

He would mark her soon, when he was done with his run, and had bathed. The girl needed something concrete to hold her, mentally, to her situation. If she continued thinking of every moment as one moment closer to her freedom, she'd never be present fully enough with him to learn to love him.

A beautiful deer caught his scent. It was hidden just yonder behind a tree. The Beast paused, one arm off the ground, ready to turn and give chase. The deer sensed the predator that he was and ran, its spindly legs moving so fast they seemed a blur. But the Beast was faster. Breathing hard, he caught up with the animal, his hind legs bent, ready to pounce.

But something stopped him. An image of the expression on Belle's face, if she were to see him hunting with his bare hands and teeth, ran through his mind. He was not an animal, he was not a monster. Beneath his beastly exterior, he was a man. He was Frederick.

And Frederick wanted to be with Belle more than the Beast wanted to kill a helpless deer.

The Beast paused, panting, and turned back to the castle. Instead of running on all fours like he usually did, he walked back on his legs, like a gentleman. The deer ran out of sight, not trusting this turn of events. No matter. When the Beast reached the castle, he would call upon a supper to be laid out for him. He could even request venison if he so desired. But there was no need to tear the meat from that beautiful creature's flesh. No need to behave like a beast, even if that was what he'd become.

Once, he was a prince. He could never be a prince again, but he could be a man. For Belle.

For Belle, he would do anything.

Back in the library, a note drifted from the air on a piece of paper, and landed neatly on top of the copy of Voltaire's scandalous *Candide* that Belle had discovered. She picked the paper up in surprise, even as she noted that the sun was now low in the sky toward the west.

~~~

Please do me the honor of joining me in the East Wing sitting room. I am prepared to mark you, and I trust you are prepared to accept my invitation. As always, I shall never harm you, Beauty.

With Devotion,

The Beast

~~~

Belle folded the paper in half with trembling fingers and used it as a bookmark for her book. She set it down by the windowsill, not wanting to waste even a moment by putting it back on the shelf.

The Beast would never harm her. She could trust him. And so she went, without delay, to meet him. The castle was huge and maze-like, but sconces lit up along the walls as she walked, showing her the way.

The Beast wasn't in the sitting room in the East wing when she arrived. What should she do with herself? What would the Beast prefer?

He liked it when she knelt for him, so she carefully arranged her gown around her and waited, kneeling, head bowed.

Belle could hear his heavy footsteps prowling closer before he spoke. "You are a sight to behold, Beauty."

Raising her head to meet his gaze, Belle offered him a shaky smile. "Thank you, Sir."

And then, as if he could see past her brave façade and into her heart, he added, "You needn't be afraid. Not of me."

"I'm not," she lied quickly. "I mean… I know I needn't be, Sir, because I trust you." And that was the truth.

"Let me help you out of your gown." The Beast came closer to her, so close she felt the fur that covered his muscles brush against her bare arms. With quick hands that weren't nearly as clumsy as she would have imagined such large hands would be, he loosened the stays in her dress and, perhaps with a bit of fairy magic, managed to have her completely naked within moments.

"Sir?"

He smiled, and she clung to his arm. "Are you going to cane me?" she asked.

"I'm sure I will, at some point. But not right now."

Good Lord in Heaven, what did he have planned? The not knowing was killing her. And she had thought she had it all figured out, based on Frederick's diary. Fool, her.

The Beast took her chin with his hand and tilted her head up to him. "You need not fear my fangs, my teeth."

Before she could process what he meant, he dropped his head to her bare breast, and licked her nipple.

Oh! The sensation was almost that of a cat tongue, scratchy yet soft and wet. The sandpaper-feel of it made her nipple tighten to a hard peak, and she moaned.

"I would like to bite you, my little Beauty," he murmured.

Fear ran through her body, and every tiny hair on her flesh stood on end. But she said nothing. If the Beast said she need not fear his fangs, then she would trust him.

"Please don't hurt me," she whispered, feeling shamed as a whimper tore from her throat.

He licked her breast again, all the way around the small, pink areola, and she shuddered with pleasure.

"I won't harm you," he promised. "But it will hurt. Let the pain mingle with the pleasure. This is not a punishment, Beauty. I want you to learn to enjoy this."

With that, he nodded, and though he didn't speak, she knew what he meant. She lay back, her skin against the rich carpet that covered the stone in the sitting room, and stared up at the Beast.

He was so big, so immense—he took up her entire field of vision. Somehow, even though she was naked and vulnerable beneath him, she was no longer frightened. His face was kind. How had she not noticed the similarity in his bone structure to that of Frederick? The cheeks, the jaw... the eyes. So human. So... Frederick.

"You are magnificent, Beast," she said.

"As are you." His head brushed the insides of her spread thighs.

And then, he licked her, his thick tongue opening her nether lips to touch her very center, lapping at her bud. The scent of her heady arousal mixed with that of the fresh-cut roses throughout the sitting room, and she breathed it in, her passion mounting.

Every lick of the Beast's tongue brought on another wave of ecstasy. She writhed beneath him, moaning with desire.

Yes, oh Heavens. Yes.

Just as she reached the brink of climax, his fangs pierced her inner thigh, and she screamed as her orgasm wracked her body. The pain and the pleasure, the licking comingled with the bite, all came to a head, and she let herself fall over the cliff of sensual pleasure as she came harder than she ever had before.

The Beast held her against the carpet, running his tongue over the sensitive bite mark, lapping up the two tiny drops of scarlet blood as she shuddered through an aftershock of her orgasm.

Finally, he pulled her naked body into his arms, and cradled her against his massive chest.

She looked down at her thigh, at the pale white skin marked now with his fangs, and smiled. "The mark of the Beast," she murmured.

"Does it feel real, now, Belle?" he asked tenderly.

"It does. Thank you, Sir."

"Thank you for trusting me." The Beast nuzzled his head against hers, and their lips met for the first time since she came to his hidden castle.

Everything she had feared was for naught. His mouth on hers was heaven on earth, and everything she desired in that moment. She could faintly taste her own blood on his lips, and her arousal as well. Their tongues danced together, but his sharp teeth never scratched her. Belle had been kissed before—that time with the baker's apprentice in the hay loft—but that had been nothing compared to this.

She could kiss the Beast forever and be happy, wrapped in his huge, strong arms, so warm, so safe in his embrace.

Belle had been marked by the Beast. Now she was ravenous for more—for whatever the Beast wanted to do with her, to take from her, to give to her.

She was ready.

8

THE HORSE AND CARRIAGE

Some time had passed, when Belle lay in her suite on the cool, white linen sheets. She was still not quite sleepy despite her hot bath, and ran her fingers over the Beast's mark on her inner thigh. Light purple bruises had blossomed at first around the bite like an old sailor's faded tattoo, but the mark was healed now, leaving behind the pale red mesh of new skin.

She found herself hoping it would leave a permanent scar, one that would forever remind her of her time with the Beast. Two tiny, perfectly circular dots scarring her pale skin. Yes, that was what she wanted. It would be beautiful, like the Beast himself.

Beautiful. Was that how she now perceived the Beast? How had such an enormous perception shift occurred in so short a time?

Belle rose and stood in front of the armoire. She didn't want to go to sleep just yet. Perhaps if she could put on a dressing robe, she could go out and find the Beast. She found herself looking forward to their long conversations by the fire. He was a very intelligent man *(Beast)* and he seemed to be genuinely interested in her decidedly ordinary life.

Certainly, she had no stories about fairies or castles or secret princes imprisoned therein, as the Beast must, but still he listened to her tales of her childhood with her Papa, and she also enjoyed retelling some of her favorite stories from the books in his library.

Well, *her* library. The Beast had insisted it was now hers. A lovely gold plaque even adorned the library door, one that said, simply, "Beauty's Library." It made her smile whenever she looked upon it. Especially the fact that he named it for the pet name he had given her, one she was hardly deserving of… and yet, he seemed to believe she was.

"Fairies, may I have a dressing robe to cover my nightgown, please? And slippers."

The requested items appeared draped over the bed, and Belle dressed quickly.

The corridor was empty, the long, red rug spreading out before her like a river. Where was the Beast? What did he do, late at night, when she wasn't with him?

Part of her feared he might be out hunting. She'd seen him enter the castle with fresh blood on his mouth. Not recently, no, but it had happened. The thought of him hunting and killing with the same fangs that so lovingly marked her made her a bit ill.

Best not to think on it. It wasn't as if she could change the Beast into something less beastly.

"Sir?" she said aloud, hoping he would hear. No answer.

She crept down the dark corridor and descended the stairway to the main hall. The place was deserted.

"Beast, where are you?" she called again. No reply.

The front door lay just a few meters away, the only thing standing between her and freedom. She'd promised the Beast she wouldn't try to escape, and with all of the wolves prowling the forest, she knew she wouldn't make it far if she tried. Not without a horse and carriage to protect her.

But there wouldn't be much harm in merely taking in some fresh night air, right? She could just open the door and look at the stars for a while until she got sleepy enough to return to bed.

With that plan in mind, Belle touched the door, and pulled. It didn't open.

Locked in. Of course. She was, after all, the Beast's prisoner. As much as he tried to make her comfortable and at home, if she couldn't leave when she wished, she was only a well-pampered captive. Not a guest.

"Fairies," she whispered, surprised by the urgency in her voice. "Open the door."

The door opened, and the cool night air rushed in to the front hall to greet her. How glorious! She hadn't been outside, in nature, since that horrible night she almost got ripped to shreds by the wolves. The night the Beast spanked her for nearly getting herself killed. *And for cutting him*, she amended.

Belle stepped outside, wrapping her robe tightly around her. The moon and stars lit up the sky magnificently, and she gazed on them with wonder. Was her Papa looking up at the same sky, thinking of her, as she was of him? Maybe he was, right at this moment.

"If you can hear me, Papa," she said softly, "I will come home to you soon." She paused thoughtfully, imagining the night, in only a few more months, that she would be set free. "I'll have a horse and carriage to lead me safely through the woods and home to you, and I will get there as fast as I can. I promise, Papa."

At her words, a horse-drawn carriage appeared at the front drive, finely appointed with plush cushions inside, and thick wooden sides that would keep her safe from the predators in the woods.

"Oh my word," she gasped. She looked around the empty landscape. "Fairies, what have you done?"

She hadn't meant to make a wish. She hadn't meant to ask the fairies to help her escape. But in speaking her desire out loud, Belle had summoned the fairies into being accomplices in her betrayal.

That was what leaving the Beast would be—a betrayal. She had promised him six months of servitude without him needing to fear she would escape, in lieu of a lifetime in his dungeon. If the Beast came back to the castle now and saw the horse and carriage, he would be furious. Even worse, he would be…heartbroken.

"I didn't mean for this to happen," she whispered.

But it had. And if she chose, she could hop right into that carriage and leave the castle, the fairies, Frederick, and the Beast behind.

She'd never have to see them again. Ever.

Belle took a step toward the carriage, her heart racing. The wind picked up and blew straight through the thin silk of her dressing robe, and she shivered. Escape was but a few steps away.

But she hesitated. Why? Here was her chance at freedom! She could go, now. She could be gone before the Beast even knew she was missing. He would think she was asleep in her suite, and not even look for her until morning.

Frederick would know, when he couldn't find her in her dreams (because she doubted she could sleep as the carriage took her through the treacherous forest), but what could a man who only existed in her dreams do to her?

Nothing. If she chose to leave, she'd be safe. Somehow, after all this time together with the Beast, she felt he cared for her too much to make good on his threat to find her and eat her if she ran away. She could go home tonight and be at her Papa's side once more.

There was only one problem with her plan.

Belle didn't want to leave the Beast.

Yes, she wanted to be with her Papa again, and she hated the thought of betraying her word to the Beast by escaping. She also hated the thought of how brokenhearted the Beast might feel upon learning that he'd been made a fool for trusting her.

But the primary reason she couldn't seem to take another step toward that carriage, toward her freedom, was that she wanted to spend more time with the Beast (and Frederick, if she were honest with herself). There was still so much to learn from him, so much to share with him.

She was afraid of the Beast, but she cared about him as well. Both the Beast, and Frederick. Seeing them both, the beast and the man, was the highlight of her long days.

If she went back home, she'd be going back to her simple, boring life, as quiet and sweet as it had been. Belle wasn't certain she'd be happy if she couldn't walk the halls of the grand castle, exploring its secrets and frightening herself near to death every time she rounded a corner and ran into her massive, monstrous, handsome beast.

"Go away," she said, her voice cracking. "Fairies, please, take the horse and carriage away, before the Beast returns. I don't want to leave tonight."

Maybe tomorrow night she'd change her mind, or the night after that. But right now, what she really wanted was to stay at the castle. With the knowledge that she could leave at anytime if she simply summoned up the means to do so, she was no longer the Beast's captive.

For the first time, Belle truly felt like an honored guest. Even more, the castle was beginning to feel like it could be home, in its own way. Not home like the warm little cottage she shared with her father, no, but the warmth in the castle came from the heat the Beast created within her. The fire.

The horse and carriage disappeared as quickly as it had arrived, leaving behind only the shimmer that freshly-sown magic always seemed to do. When the wind blew again, the shimmer dissipated into the night air.

Belle turned around and marched back through the castle

door, closing it firmly behind her. She stared at the open expanse of the great hall, and breathed in the scent of cut roses, the bouquets that adorned every flat surface imaginable.

"I do believe I am ready for sleep, now," she said aloud.

Perhaps Frederick would hear her, in some other plane or dimension, and he would meet her in her bedchamber.

Belle smiled and danced up the stairs to her suite.

At the edge of the forest, hidden from view, the Beast watched silently as Belle's chance at escape disappeared into the night. He exhaled slowly, not even realizing he'd been holding his breath, awaiting her decision.

She had chosen to stay. The very fact humbled him.

The relief was indescribable. After their rocky start, he'd almost lost all hope of getting Belle to care for him, to be able to look at him and see something other than a monster.

"Thank you, Beauty," he whispered, his words lost in the blowing wind.

He wanted to go inside and reward her for her loyalty, but after a long night of fruitless hunting, he was so exhausted that he might have to fall asleep and meet her as Frederick in his dreams, instead.

The animals in the forest, like Belle, were less afraid of him now, which should have afforded him even more chances to kill. But instead, he found himself watching their beauty from afar, and he couldn't bring himself to hurt the creatures—not anymore. He was a changed man.

Maybe this was what the enchantress had meant, all along. That a woman could change him from a beast back into a man. He certainly felt more human than he ever had in the past ten years since the curse struck him.

But it wasn't just a woman that he needed. He needed true love.

For the first time since he found Belle, love seemed like a very real possibility. He still had a chance.

They had a chance.

Later that evening, Belle awoke to the sound of her bedchamber door creaking open. She sat up, holding the white linen bedding up against her breasts, blinking until her eyes adjusted to the dark.

"Frederick?"

"Good evening, Beauty," Frederick said softly. "May I sit with you?"

Belle smiled and patted the space on the bed next to her. She had no guilt or shame about inviting Frederick into her bed, after all, he was her dream-man, her fantasy, and she fully intended to make good use of him.

Even if he was possibly a little bit real.

"Fairies, some candlelight, please?" she requested.

Candles flickered to life throughout her bedroom, illuminating Frederick's handsome face as he sat beside her.

"I'm glad you stayed," Frederick said. "I would have missed you terribly if you'd left."

"Now I know I must be dreaming," she said, uncertain if she felt relief or disappointment. "Because no one knows what happened earlier other than the fairies. And me."

Frederick grinned and cupped her face in his warm, large hands, pulling her in closer for a kiss. She opened her mouth to him, accepting his tongue, and, in a moment of reckless abandon, pulled him on top of her body.

"I thought you said we couldn't make love," Frederick reminded her. "The Beast would know."

"I belong to the Beast," she agreed. "Look, he marked me." She proudly displayed her bite mark, spreading her legs lewdly beneath him.

"The Beast deserves to have you first, before I do. Are you ready for that? To make love with the Beast?"

Belle swallowed hard. The thought both terrified and aroused her. "Yes. I am."

Frederick dropped his hand between her legs, finding her wetness there. Carefully, slowly, he penetrated her with his finger. First one, then two. Then three.

Belle moaned as she stretched, but she didn't try to stop him. She knew what Frederick was doing.

He was preparing her for the Beast.

"Aren't you jealous, Frederick?" she whispered, moaning as he circled his fingers, lubricating her with her own juices. "Don't you care for me at all?"

"I can't explain, Beauty," he said. "But I've said from the start that you must love the Beast."

"But what if I love you?"

She covered her mouth with her hand, shocked by the words that had fallen out of her, seemingly of their own volition.

"Is your heart big enough to love me, and the Beast?" he asked.

The prospect had never occurred to her. Frederick and the Beast were like two sides of the same coin, one refined and handsome, the other brutal and beastly. And yet she desired them both.

She didn't know how to respond, so she did something she'd never done before—she reached toward his erection, and dropped her head to his lap, wanting to kiss him there the way he had done to her.

Frederick grinned. "What are you doing?"

"I honestly have no idea," she said, opening his trousers.

His cock was thick, heavy in her hand, and glistened at the end with a drop of arousal. Belle lowered her head and licked the drop off, savoring the taste of salt and man. Had she ever been able to taste something in a dream before?

"Is this all right?" she asked.

"Open your mouth," he said. "Take it all in, lick with your tongue, and try to keep your teeth at bay."

Belle hesitated for only a moment before wrapping her lips around his cock. The heat of it, the taste of his flesh in her mouth, was so fantastical and new that she murmured in delight, causing Frederick to moan with pleasure, and tangle his hands in her long hair.

She continued tonguing his cock, swallowing around it, and looked up at him to see if he was enjoying himself. Frederick was so beautiful, with that thick, brown hair, and deep green eyes, eyes that were half-closed now with pleasure.

"I need to know, Beauty," he said, his voice rough with desire, "can you love the Beast? Can you love us both?"

It made no sense. What man would want her to love another man? But the truth was, when she had her chance for freedom, it wasn't just one man she thought of that kept her from leaving. It was both the man, and the Beast. So yes. Yes, she could, perhaps, someday…love them both.

"I think so," she said, sitting up.

Frederick groaned and took hold of her hand, guiding it over his cock. With his hand over hers, he rubbed himself, faster and faster, until he cried out, his face in a grimace that looked almost

(beastly)

primal, and come flowed out of his cock, pouring hotly over her hand.

"Thank you, Belle," Frederick said.

He rose and washed with water from the basin, and she watched intently, enjoying the view. His long, lean muscled body, the way his strong jawline gleamed in the candlelight…

"You're so handsome, Frederick."

For some reason, he stiffened. "It shouldn't matter what I look like. I want you to love me for who I am, inside."

"You're a fantasy. I've made you up in my dreams."

"I may be in your dreams, Belle, but I am as real as my diary, as real as my portrait."

She gasped. "How did you know I found your old diary?"

"You were looking for me in the castle. It's all right, I suppose it's one way you could get to know me. Although I hope you understand I've grown as a person a lot in the last ten years, since I kept that diary."

Ten years. The same ten years that he'd been missing from the castle. The same ten years ago that the Beast told her he'd changed.

But nothing made sense, and none of her past experiences ever showed her a way that two men could be one, and so she dismissed the niggling thoughts that threatened to break her very sanity.

Frederick was for her dreams, the Beast was for her reality, as strange as it might be.

"You need to wake up, now, darling," Frederick said.

"I don't want to wake up."

He walked back over to the bed and, in an instant, had her over his knee.

"Wh-what?" she cried, although secretly, she'd been wanting Frederick to make good on his promise to spank her.

His hand came down hard on her bare buttocks, and she gasped at the sudden sting of his palm.

"Are you ready for the Beast?" he asked, spanking her again.

She couldn't focus on what Frederick was saying, because all of her thoughts flew from her mind as he spanked her, warming her bottom, and he kept saying…

"You need to wake up, Beauty. It's time to be with the Beast."

9

SUBMITTING TO THE BEAST

Belle woke up with her face against her pillow, her bottom burning, her inner thighs wet with arousal. She felt tender, inside, where Frederick had stretched her with his long fingers.

But Frederick was gone, and the dream was over.

She rolled over and pulled the covers up to her chin, staring at the flickering candles, half-melted in their holders. At least an hour or two must have passed for the candles to have burned down like that.

Had that experience with Frederick really happened? Or was it, once again, but a dream?

There was a hard knock on her bedroom door.

"Frederick?" she whispered.

"Beauty," the Beast's voice answered. "It is I. The Beast. May I enter?"

Belle got out of bed and wrapped herself in her dressing robe, then opened the door. The Beast stood in her doorframe, his enormous body taking up the entire space, blocking any escape to the corridor outside her suite.

Why think of escape?

Because she was frightened. As much as she had imagined this moment, and even after talking about it with Frederick, she was still afraid of losing her virginity.

She was, once again, afraid of the Beast.

"Did I wake you?" he asked.

Belle shook her head mutely, but gestured that he should enter. He did, standing just inside the door, and it shut behind him on its own.

"Are you frightened, Beauty?" the Beast asked, and she ran into his arms, pressing her face against his muscled abdomen, for he was so, so tall.

He wrapped his arms around, comforting her, and she finally found the strength to tilt her chin up to look at his fearsome face.

"Yes, Beast. I am frightened. But I want to give myself to you, I do…" she smiled, even as a single errant tear rolled down her cheek.

He touched her cheek gently, wiping the tear away. "I've waited until it seemed you were ready for this. Ready for me."

"I know," she said. "Thank you for that. I know you could have…I mean, you had me captive, in your dungeon. You didn't have to be so gentle with me, and I appreciate that you are."

"Beauty," he said, his voice low, "you have come to mean everything to me. I wouldn't do anything to harm you, not for the world."

"Can I…can I see it? See…you?" Heat warmed her cheeks, and she knew she was blushing. Could he tell, in the low light, how nervous she was?

She worried that he would laugh at her request—or worse, not know what she meant, but the Beast nodded, strands of hair from his mane falling in front of his intense green eyes. He stepped back slightly, and she missed the contact with his body immediately.

Belle turned her head, in an attempt to provide him some sort of privacy as he reached for his trousers, but it seemed that he was as unsure of himself now as she was.

After her experience with Frederick's manhood, the warm, hard, veined cock that had so recently been in her mouth (*or not, if it had been a dream…had it been a dream?*), Belle wasn't sure what to expect.

The Beast lowered his trousers and stepped out of them, and she focused on the floor, on the wolves' paws he called feet, at the muscled calves and thighs. She brought her gaze higher, and took in a shaky breath.

His cock swung low between his legs, almost as thick as her forearm, it seemed. As she looked upon him, he became erect, his cock stiffening and growing even as she watched. It was a beautiful, terrible thing to behold, and she touched it with her fingertips to see if it differed too much from Frederick's cock.

It felt the same, warm, velvety skin, and the thick veins that ran across the Beast's cock stood out in stark relief. Her hands trembled as she touched him there, as his cock became like a steel rod encased in flesh.

"Beast," she whispered. "This won't fit inside of me. You'll tear me in two."

To her dismay, a sob escaped her throat. All this waiting, all this time, and she'd never even get to experience having the Beast make love to her.

"No, Beauty," he said, "I won't tear you. We'll go slowly and carefully, and you'll be fine. A woman's channel can stretch to accommodate even a baby, and while I know I am well-endowed, we're nowhere near that."

She looked up at him in trepidation. "Do you really think I'll be okay?"

"I wouldn't do it if I thought differently."

The Beast picked her up, holding her so that her lips met his, and she melted into his strong embrace. As they kissed, he captured her clitoris with his fingers, and rubbed slow, lazy circles on her tender bud until she began to relax and enjoy herself.

Soon his fingers were inside her, so much bigger than Frederick's fingers had been, but he did exactly the same thing her dream-lover had done, carefully stretching her, rubbing the inside of her channel, lubricating every bit of her with her own arousal.

Belle panted with desire; he kept hitting that spot deep within her that had made her come so hard before, and she felt another climax building. She waited for him to stop, to pull away before she came too soon, but he kept going, holding her thighs apart, pushing her back onto the bed, and pleasuring her until she melted, wave after wave of her orgasm flowing through her body.

The Beast ran his hand over her sensitive cunny, and covered his cock with her come, until it glistened in the candlelight. A few candles had burnt out completely, she half-noted, he had spent so much time preparing her body for him.

"You won't...crush me, will you?" she asked.

The Beast had to weigh over three hundred pounds, maybe four hundred, and she had no experience other than the feel of Frederick's strong body lying on hers.

"Never. It will be easier if I can stand," he said. "Come here, Beauty."

He positioned her body, bent over the side of the bed, and gently pulled her robe off of her, letting it drop to the floor. Naked, she trembled, waiting for him. Her nipples pebbled against the bedsheets, her fingers grabbed hold of the linen and tightened in anticipation.

The Beast stood behind her, and pressed a sweet kiss to her cheek. None of his weight was on her, and she exhaled shakily.

"You are everything to me, Beauty," he whispered. "Is this all right? You don't have to do this."

"Yes, Beast," she said. "I want this. I need this."

He pressed his cock to the entrance of her cunny, and she moaned, still fearful of how it would feel. Slowly, carefully, he entered her, stretching her wet heat, filling her completely. His cock rubbed against every nerve ending in her body, mingling pain and pleasure in almost the same way as his lovebite had done when he'd marked her.

She cried out as he pulled back and slowly thrust inside of her once more.

"It's all right, little Beauty, everything's all right," he whispered, his voice low and rumbling.

Her whole world narrowed until nothing existed except for the Beast inside of her, stroking her, touching every part of her from the inside out.

It seemed to go on forever, and yet she didn't want it to end. Her pleasure bloomed and rose on crest after crest of waves of sensation, and she bit the pillow, stifling her own cries of passion.

But the Beast ripped the pillow from her mouth. "I want to hear you, Beauty. I want to hear you scream with pleasure."

He pulled out of her, leaving her empty, wanting. She cried out inarticulately in protest—

Don't stop!

—but he lifted her from the bed like she weighed nothing at all, and held her in his arms. Her legs wrapped around his waist as if of their own accord; she clung to him, this mountain of a man.

The Beast grabbed her thighs and raised her up and onto his cock, impaling her with delicious passion. Belle threw her head back in ecstasy and held on for dear life.

"Yes, Beast, yes," she moaned, unable—unwilling—to contain herself any longer.

She grabbed his bulging muscles, wanting to feel all of him, to experience everything about him. She tore at his hair, pulling his face toward hers for a long, deep kiss. Then, in a moment of primal abandon, she bit his mouth, as if daring him to bite her back.

With a low growl, he threw her onto the bed on her back. Belle cried out in surprise—he was so tall, the drop to the bed was five or six feet at least. He loomed over her, his beautiful green eyes dark with lust and desire.

"I'm sorry, Sir—" she whispered, even though, if given half a chance, she'd do it again.

"Never be sorry, Beauty."

He braced himself above her, his body inches from hers, supported by his own arms and legs.

"I won't crush you," he rumbled. "I won't hurt you."

"I trust you, Sir," she said.

She did, with all her heart.

The sight of him hovering above her was terrifying indeed, but at the same time aroused her deepest passion. She moaned with pleasure as he thrust inside her once more.

Belle wrapped her arms around him, the heat of his breath warm on her bare neck. His thrusts shook her to the core, awakening her entire body.

She gave him the screams he wanted, her passion mounting even as she felt she would be torn apart by his power. Belle knew she was safe with him, and her fear only intensified her arousal.

The Beast sped up his pace, rocking within her, moving faster, faster, until he came with a loud roar that shook the chandelier and made the lights flicker. Belle whimpered and nearly scrambled to get out from under him, her natural instinct overtaking her, despite desperately wanting

(needing)

more. And more. She cried out, her desire echoing through the bedchamber.

He held her hips, pinning her to the bed, wrenching another

delicious orgasm from deep within her.

It's like when Frederick came, how he seemed more animal than man. In that moment of pure ecstasy, he had been reduced to his most primal instincts.

The Beast pulled out, hot come splattering on her breasts. She lay still, not daring to move, breathing hard.

"Stay still, Beauty. Let me tend to you."

She closed her eyes, nearly drifting off into sleep, when she felt the warm, wet towel wiping her skin, cleaning her off. The Beast placed tender kisses on her body as he dropped to his knees at the bedside and washed between her legs. His face was so close to her there, inspecting her.

"You're perfect," he said. "You didn't even bleed."

"I fell off a horse when I was a child," she said, "and bled then. So my maidenhood was already torn. But I swear I was a virgin for you, Sir."

The Beast smiled at her, and laid down in the bed next to her. His weight made the mattress sink a bit, and she rolled next to his body, cuddling up to him.

"I never doubted you were a virgin, Belle," he said, "but that doesn't matter to me. I care about who you are now, not what you might have done in the past."

"I care about who you are, too," she whispered. "And not about what you might have done in the past."

Images of him coming back to the castle late at night, fresh from a kill, haunted her, but she pushed them back. He was changed.

"Beauty, I never thought I'd be lucky enough to find you. But I'm a monster for how I've kept you against your will. I know you miss your father, and that you want to see him."

Belle froze, uncertain what to say, or what to do. Of course she wanted to see her father, but she also didn't want to leave the Beast (*or Frederick*).

The two wants conflicted horribly.

"I have a way for you to see your Papa, Belle," the Beast said softly. "Would you like that?"

Belle hesitated. Was this a trick? But no, her Beast had never tricked her, never lied to her. So she nodded.

"I need the looking glass," Beast said, to the fairies, she presumed.

In his hand appeared an ornate, hand-held looking glass. It was beautiful. Belle smiled wistfully. Yes, she knew she looked a bit like her Papa, but viewing her reflection in a mirror was not quite the same as seeing her father. Still, the Beast was attempting to show her kindness, so she was willing to cooperate, if only to please him.

"Here, Beauty," he said, lying next to her, cuddled on the bed. He handed her the mirror (which was surprisingly heavy) and she held it up, gazing into it. "Tell the looking glass what you want to see, and it will show you."

"I want... I want to see my Papa," she whispered.

The looking glass hazed over, as if she'd breathed on it while outside on a winter day, and then as if the summer sun hit the glass, it cleared, and she saw... *her Papa!*

"Oh Lord in Heaven," she gasped. "Papa, Papa can you hear me?"

"He can't hear you, nor see you," the Beast said. "It is just a way for you to view him. If you listen carefully, you might be able to hear him if he speaks, as well."

"He looks terrible," she said sadly.

Her Papa was lying in an unfamiliar bed, staring at the ceiling with wide, vacant eyes. One of his wrists, she saw now, was chained to the bedrail at his side.

"Oh, Papa, what have they done to you?" she wailed. "He must have gone insane with worry for me."

Then one of Constable's men walked into the room her Papa was being kept in, and unlocked the chain. Her Papa stood, unsteady on his feet, and bowed his head.

"I didn't kill my daughter," he said to the floor. The officer took no notice.

"The people will decide your fate, Mr. Castelle," the man said. "You don't need to try and convince me. Belle is missing, and feared dead. Who else but you, with your crazy stories of a Beast, would have committed such a terrible, unnatural crime?"

Belle touched the glass, wishing she could transcend through it and into the room with them, to show them that she was here, she was alive!

"Beast," she said turning to him, frantic. "I need to get my Papa out of there! If the Constable can just see that I am well, not murdered, then he will have no choice but to free my father."

The Beast took the mirror from her hands and set it down, his anguished expression nearly matching her own.

"I don't know what to say, Belle. I thought seeing your Papa would bring you joy… I didn't mean for this to happen."

"But it did," she whispered. "It happened."

"I didn't realize that they would charge him with crimes he didn't commit." He paused, for a long moment, as if turning the options over in his head.

"If you let me go make this right, I will return within a week, I swear on my life."

The Beast winced as if he'd been slapped. "No, Belle. No. You mustn't say that."

"But I do swear, Beast, I do!"

When something like that is spoken inside an enchanted castle, the castle listens. The castle would make it happen.

"No!" he roared, for Belle did not realize the power of her promise. "Swear on *my* life, Beauty. Swear on *my life* instead." The Beast's words were seeped in desperation.

"Please, Beast, Sir, please," she begged. "Let me go to him. Give me your blessing."

But the Beast grabbed hold of her hand, as if to keep her

there forever.

"Beast," she whispered gravely. "I swear on…" she hesitated. "…On your life, Sir, that I will return within the week. *I swear to it.*"

He exhaled and let her hand go.

"I need… I need a moment to think, Belle." He stood. "I'm going for a walk to clear my head. You will have your answer when I return." The Beast took her hand in his, caressed it, and let it go. "Will you be waiting for me when I come back? Can I trust you?"

"Yes, Beast. I will be here."

She couldn't help the tears that flowed down her cheeks. If she didn't stay, if she chose to escape without his blessing, he would never trust her again. And their relationship had grown to the point where losing his trust would break her very heart.

"I *will* be here, Beast. Go for your walk." Belle rolled over, burying her face in the pillow, and sobbed.

She heard her bedroom door shut quietly behind the Beast.

The Beast ran out of the castle, bounding across the castle grounds on all fours, sweeping past the trees on the edge of the forest, and kept running through the woods until he was nearly out of breath.

He stopped, stood, and leaned against a tree, allowing it to support his massive weight.

Making love with Beauty had been the most intense, wonderful experience of his life. Not just in his life as the Beast, but in his entire life, including when he was still a Prince. Nothing else even came close.

He thought he'd loved Nadine, back then, and maybe he did. But sex with her was mere fucking. Sex with Belle was love. Pure love.

I'm in love with Belle, my little Beauty!

The thought struck the breath from him, and he gazed heavenward, wondering at the goodness of it all, and how wonderful life could be.

It was clear, though, that she didn't love him back. Not yet. If she did, her kiss would have broken the curse, and he would be back in human form once more already. But he was still a Beast.

How could he love her, but keep her all to himself, away from her Papa in his time of need? If her father was convicted for her murder, while all the time the Beast was keeping her secreted away in his castle, she would be heartbroken. Miserable. And most likely, unable to ever see the Beast as anything but pure evil.

A delicate fawn crossed his path, ambling by so close he could almost touch her. She was so tiny, so fragile, so beautiful. The Beast could destroy that fawn immediately if he so desired. Mere months ago, he would have thought nothing of doing just that.

But now, he knelt on the forest floor, and waited patiently for the fawn to come closer. She looked at him with her big brown eyes and skitted forward, as though unsure whether or not to trust a Beast who wasn't on the hunt.

"It's all right, baby, you're safe near me," the Beast whispered.

The fawn came closer, and nudged his big hand with her warm, soft nose. The Beast smiled and ran his hand over her silky head, rubbing her ears. The fawn closed her eyes and nuzzled into his touch. Even though he was bigger, stronger, and dangerous, the fawn trusted him with her life, and took comfort from him.

Dear God... He had to let Belle go.

The Beast gave the fawn a final pat in the head, and headed back to the castle. Back up the stairs into Belle's suite, back into her bedchamber.

She lay on her bed, her cheeks wet with tears, her eyes

swollen from crying. Even in this state, she was the most beautiful woman he'd ever seen.

"Belle," he whispered, and she looked up at him. "You may go see your Papa, with my blessing. Clear his name. But…if you don't return in a week, *I will die*."

"I promise, Beast, I will return. You have my word."

With a heavy sigh, the Beast helped Belle up from the bed, and wiped away her tears. "Bring the looking glass with you, so you can see me, and not forget me." He opened his palm and said to the castle air, "I need the ring."

A thick, golden ring with a ruby the size of a grape glistening in its setting, as beautiful and crimson as a rose, appeared magically in his large hand. The air shimmered for a moment between them, then all was normal again.

"Take this ring with you, Beauty." He pressed it into her small palm, and she wrapped her fingers around it to keep it safe. "When you are ready to return, simply put the ring on, and twist it around fully three times. You will be transported instantly back to the castle. Back to me."

Belle nodded, clearly desperate to go save her father.

He took the ring from her hand and put it on her finger. Staring deep into her eyes, he turned the ring. Once, twice.

"Go now, Beauty, and Godspeed."

Three times, and she was gone.

10

HOME AND HEARTH

Belle felt the air around her get warm, no… hot, burning hot, and suddenly, the Beast was gone, the castle gone. The air around her shimmered brightly, and then any hint of magic disappeared around her. All was normal.

She stood now in her Papa's little cottage, standing in the middle of the cozy kitchen.

"Oh, my word," she gasped. How quickly the magic had worked! To be transported through space like that, how strange, how wonderful. She was *home*.

Belle ran into her father's bedroom, hoping upon hope that he was already safe and free. But the room was empty, the fire out, the ashes unswept.

She took off the golden ruby ring and set it on the center of her father's dresser top. God forbid if she wore it outside and a thief stole it from her, she might have a hard time getting back through the long, winding way in the dark forest to the castle. Would she even know the way? And if she did, would wolves tear her to shreds before she could make it back to her beloved

Beast?

In her bedroom, she set the looking glass down on her bed. Belle dressed quickly in one of her old, worn dresses, and put on sturdy shoes. She had missed the smell of the house, the smell of old wood and burnt embers and Papa and home. But there was no time to reminisce. Her father was in danger, and she was his only hope.

With no time to spare, she left the cottage, running to the Constable as fast as she could.

When she finally reached the Constable's office, she burst through the door. The man was sitting at his desk, going through paperwork. Both of the tiny holding cells were empty. Where was her father?

"Constable," she nearly shouted. "It has come to my attention that you have charged my father with my murder. As you can see, I am alive and well. My father is innocent and I demand he be set free at once."

The Constable stood so quickly that his chair fell over, the noise clattering through the room like a shot.

"Good God, girl!" he exclaimed. "We all thought you dead! Where have you been?"

"I've been staying with a dear friend, a friend with…" she paused, unsure how to continue. "He has a deformity, and my father, with his weak eyesight, mistook him for a beast in his, um, fur coat. As you can see, I am unharmed."

"I can't believe this," he said, coming over to her. He touched her arm, as if to ascertain that she was, indeed, alive and real.

It reminded Belle of how she felt when she first saw Frederick. The uncertainty of it all, the confusion.

"Take me to my Papa," she said. "Please, Constable. I need to see him."

"Very well." He looked at her again, shaking his head in amazement. "My goodness, of course. Right away."

The Constable led her to his carriage, and they sat together, side by side, as the horse clopped along the hard-packed dirt road to the Institution for Lunatics.

"Mrs. Sharone is the one who needs to decide whether or not he is well enough to go home," he warned. "I can drop the criminal charges, naturally—I must, it seems. Of course, I must. Can't charge a man for murder when his victim is not dead."

"No, you cannot," Belle said, unable to hide her anger.

"But, well, Mr. Castelle is still being treated for his hallucinations and delusions."

"There are no hallucinations or delusions," Belle said firmly. "Only a misunderstanding. I will bring my Papa home with me, and I can guarantee he won't be a nuisance to anyone at all."

The Constable nodded, and they rode the rest of the way in silence.

At the Institution, Mrs. Sharone greeted her husband at the door, but gasped, covering her mouth with her hand, when she saw Belle step out from his carriage.

"Good Heavens!" she cried. "Belle Castelle! We all feared the worst, my poor dear, are you all right?"

"I'm perfectly fine," Belle said calmly, though inside she raged, and was quite desperate to see her Papa. "Where is he? Take me to him at once, I beg you!"

"Certainly, my dear, come with me."

As they navigated the maze of corridors and sterile white walls, the locked doors with tiny barred viewing windows in each, Mrs. Sharone finally stopped in front of one.

"Oh dear," she muttered under her breath.

"What is it?" Belle asked. *What have they done with my Papa?*

"Mr. Ashley already took him to prepare for the courthouse. I forgot the time, I've been so busy..." Mrs. Sharone's voice trailed off.

"How could you not know your own patient's whereabouts?"

Belle fumed. "And you, Constable, how could you not know he was going to court today?"

"Now, now, Belle," he said, as if to calm her (which only infuriated her more). "My job is to protect our village. It is up to the lawyers and the judge to see to the other side of things."

"Bring me to my father!" Belle struggled to keep her voice even, to not scream, lest they lock her up herself for hysteria.

"At once, of course, don't you worry," the Constable said. To his wife, he said, "Belle has informed me that it seems Mr. Castelle's delusions are based on a misunderstanding."

"His poor vision made him see a beast," Belle said, the lies falling easily off her tongue, "when it was merely a man in a fur coat, a man with a horrible deformity. I've been staying with this man outside of town to assist him." She had no intention of telling them that there really was a Beast. "So we must get my Papa home with me at once. I need your help, Mrs. Sharone, and Constable, sir. I need you to testify that Henry Castelle is neither criminal nor insane."

Mrs. Sharone looked at her husband, frowning, but the Constable nodded to her, and she sighed heavily.

"I was so sure," Mrs. Sharone muttered. "Well. We must make this right, then," she said finally. "Let's not tarry."

The three went back outside to the carriage and retraced their path, back to town, and stopped outside of the courthouse. A crowd was beginning to form.

The Constable tossed a coin to one of the men to water and stable his horse while he was gone.

Belle didn't wait, she ran past them into the small courthouse. Her father stood, in chains, before the judge.

"Your honor!" she called, pushing past the crowd. "Please, your honor, I am not murdered. There has been a mistake."

Her father's face lit up. "Am I dreaming? Belle, is that really you?"

"Yes, Papa," she cried. "It's me."

She ran up to him, ignoring the shouting in the courtroom, and wrapped her arms around him. He couldn't return the embrace with his wrists chained in front of him, but he kissed her face, overjoyed to see his daughter had not been eaten by the Beast.

The Constable and his wife stepped forward, and gave their amended testimony to the judge.

The judge nodded to the officer, who stood near her father, and he took his keys out of his pocket and immediately freed him.

"You are free to go, Mr. Castelle," the judge said, "with the court's apologies. We sought justice for your daughter, but it is clear as day that she has not been murdered, nor eaten by a beast. Court is adjourned."

He banged his gavel, the sharp knock echoing through the courthouse. It sounded like freedom.

Henry Castelle hugged Belle tightly. "Thank goodness you're all right," he sobbed. "Did the Beast harm you?"

"Shhh," she said. She gripped his shoulder and spoke into her father's ear, her voice low and desperate. *"Never speak of him.* I'm fine. Let's go home, Papa."

At home, after her Papa had a long hot bath and a good rest, they sat together and she tried to explain about the Beast. But her father would have none of it.

"Please, Belle, do not speak of that monster—it breaks my heart. I just want to be with you, to make up for the time we have lost."

It had been a long, exhausting day, and here at home, there was no Beast to seek out for relaxing conversation.

She longed for Frederick, as well. The sooner she lay her head on her pillow, the sooner she might see him. At least with Frederick, she could talk about the Beast to her heart's content.

After supper and reading aloud to her father for a while, they bid each other goodnight with a long, tearful embrace, and she went to her room to sleep in her own bed for the first time since she became the Beast's prisoner.

It felt good to be home, it did. But she already missed the Beast, and missed Frederick. The events of the day swirled in her mind, over and over, repeating itself endlessly, affording her no rest.

...Confronting the Constable, watching as he knocked his chair to the floor in surprise...

...The maze of doors at the mental asylum, finding her father's room vacant, not knowing where her Papa was...

...Running into the courthouse to find him in chains, embracing him, calling out for mercy on his head...

...The sound of the gavel granting her Papa his long-awaited freedom.

Oh, it had been a long day indeed. She snuck back out of her room and into the kitchen, where she found a small bottle of sherry, and took a deep swallow to help slow her circling thoughts and ease her into dreamland, where she might meet with Frederick and find comfort in his arms once more.

With the effects of the alcohol easing her mind, she tumbled back into her little bed and fell into a fitful sleep. But in her dreams, she wandered her village alone.

Where is my Frederick?

"Fairies, help me find my lover," she whispered to the night sky.

The stars looked down on her without answer. There were no fairies here.

There was no Frederick in her dreams that night, either. Perhaps Frederick truly was imprisoned in the castle, and could only be found within its stone walls.

"Frederick?" she called out. "Where are you? Can't you find me here?"

But he could not, and he did not come to her.

That night, and every night thereafter that she slept in the small cottage, she slept alone.

And so Belle and her Papa spent the days as they used to, enjoying each other's company, the warmth of home and hearth, and each other's loving presence that had been so sorely missed—the love that only a father and daughter can share.

On the seventh day, however, Belle knew her time with her Papa had come to an end. She waited as long as she could, not wanting to ruin their last moments together. Still, she had to say goodbye, so that he wouldn't fret over her disappearance.

"Papa?" she said, sitting across from him in front of the fire.

He smiled at her, and it distressed her to have to tell him she was leaving. But she must.

"As much as it pains me to leave you, Papa... I must go tonight, and return to the castle."

"The castle?" he repeated, his eyes betraying his disbelief at her words. "Back to that Beast? No! He's an animal, a monster—"

"No, Papa—"

"You are free, you are home with me! You must never go back there. I forbid it."

"It has been a week," Belle said. "I promised the Beast I would return. And...I *want* to, Papa. I want to go back."

"He'll keep you forever in his dungeon!"

"No, not the dungeon. He's given me a lovely suite, and a library even. The Beast is taking very good care of me. He cares for me, Papa. And I for him. He's good."

"He is not *good*, Belle. You have been hypnotized by his magic. He is evil."

"You are wrong, Papa—"

"I will call the Constable and have him talk sense into you, if you won't listen to reason!"

"Please, Papa, it is *you* who must listen to reason." She took a breath to steady her voice, and held his hand. "If you tell anyone, *anyone*, that there really is a beast, they will lock you back up in the asylum. I've already told Mrs. Sharone and the Constable that your weak vision made you see a beast where there was merely a deformed man wrapped in a fur."

"My vision is as clear as it ever was!" he huffed indignantly. "I know what I saw. I know what that thing is, that *Beast*. And you are *never* to return to him."

"I told them I had been staying with him to help him, and you must tell them that again."

"I will do no such thing!" His voice rose, his brow furrowed with anguish.

"I care for him, Papa."

"That castle is enchanted, darling," he said, as if he hadn't heard her, or refused to believe. "You're under a spell, you are confused. Once you're safe at home with me for a while, you'll forget all about him."

Belle dropped her face into her hands. How could she make her Papa understand?

"Oh, sweetheart," he said, stroking her hair. "I have no idea what torture you've been through at his hands. But know this—every day and every night while you've been gone, I've been in that asylum, listening to the ravings of lunatics around me, and fearing the worst."

"No, Papa…"

"I imagined you chained in that dungeon, lying on the dirty hay behind those bars. I imagined the Beast hovering over you, his teeth dripping with blood, tearing into you. I would wake up in the night screaming from my nightmares, screaming about you, about the Beast. It is no wonder they thought me insane."

"Let me ease your mind, Papa," she said softly. "Imagine me instead, dressed in a stunning gown befitting a princess, sitting happily in an enormous library filled with books upon books, reading to my heart's content. Imagine me sleeping at night on a fine feather mattress in my own suite filled with roses, with fairies seeing to my every wish. Imagine me dining with the Beast, enjoying long conversations about everything and anything. He listens to me, Papa. He *listens*. He cares."

"Has he ever hurt you, Belle?"

She couldn't reply. How could she tell her father that yes, the Beast may have hurt her, but she found herself *liking* it? How could she explain to her father that the Beast would never harm her, and that harm was different from hurt?

"He has, hasn't he." Her Papa shook his head, moaning in distress. "My poor Belle, you will never go back to that monster. You are safe now."

"Let's not speak of it anymore," she said finally. "Let's remember fondly the week we had together. I love you, Papa, but I am no longer a child. You cannot keep here against my will."

At this, her father stood. "Belle, you may be grown, but you will always be my little girl. Always. Time can't change that. When you have a child of your own, then you will understand."

Belle couldn't wait much longer. The sun was setting, the day almost done. She placed a tender kiss on her father's head, and resigned to her bedchamber to gather up what few mementos she had, to remind her of her dear father when she was back with the Beast.

It was then that she heard the click of the lock turning on her bedroom door.

"Papa?"

She ran to the door and pulled on the knob, already knowing that it wouldn't open. He had locked her in!

"Papa, please, you must let me out. You cannot keep me here like a prisoner!"

Her father's voice came back through the wooden door. "It is better I keep you as a prisoner here at home, where you will be safe, than allow you to return to the Beast."

The sun had set, the day was done. She was late, late returning to the castle! What would become of her, what would become of the Beast?

She searched her room frantically, overthrowing the bedding in her haste. If she didn't return to the Beast at once, he would think she had forgotten him, he would think she no longer cared.

Where is the golden ruby ring? How could she have misplaced an item of such utmost importance—the one thing that would get her home safely and immediately?

Home...is that what the castle, her prison, had become? Yes, yes, it was so. No longer her prison, the castle was the one place she most wanted to be. Home, with the Beast, with Frederick.

Belle picked up the Beast's looking glass, hoping against hope that its magic would still work outside the confines of the enchanted castle.

"Please, looking glass," she whispered to her own reflection. "I want to see the golden ruby ring. Where is it?"

The glass fogged up, obscuring her reflection. *Please, please, be in my room.* Then the glass cleared once more, and she found herself staring at the golden ring...sitting atop her father's dresser, in his bedroom.

It may as well have been an ocean away.

Belle ran to the door and pounded on it with all her might. Her fists bruised with her efforts, and she cried out to her Papa to let her go.

"Belle, my child," he sobbed through the door. "Don't fret so. I love you with all of my heart, I have to keep you safe, don't you see?"

"Let me go, let me go," she cried. "You don't understand!"

"Please, sweetheart, just go to sleep. Tomorrow is another day, you'll see things differently once you've slept on it."

How could she sleep? She took her hairpins and tried, in

vain, to open the lock on the door. Nothing worked. It seemed her father had blocked her only exit with something heavy, the sofa perhaps, or the kitchen table. The door would not budge.

How could he be so cruel in his kindness?

Belle finally passed out from exhaustion, leaning up against the locked door, her cheeks stained with her tears, her eyes swollen and heavy.

As dawn broke on the eighth day, the meager sunlight reaching through the one small window in her room (too small to break and climb out of, for she had already considered that option), she picked up the mirror once more.

"Show me the Beast," she whispered. Belle only prayed she wasn't too late.

For some reason, she expected to find him prowling the great hall, stalking the castle entrance, awaiting her late return. He would spank her, surely, but she didn't care. All she wanted was to be with him.

Instead, as the fogged mirror cleared, she saw the Beast lying just outside the castle door, his immense body sprawled across the stone, his heavy mane falling over his face.

His muscular chest, bared to the morning sky, was so very still.

"Beast?" she whispered, though she knew he could not hear her.

Then, a slight movement. Not much, but his chest rose and fell, a tiny bit. He was still breathing!

Thank the Lord.

His words came back to her... *If you do not return within one week, I will die.*

At the time, she thought he meant of loneliness, that he would be heartbroken and would suffer greatly. What a fool she was! In a castle filled with enchantment and magic, how could she be so blind?

The Beast was dying, literally dying, because she had broken her promise. She had sworn, sworn on her life, and he had so quickly turned it around onto his own.

She was killing him.

With renewed urgency, Belle raised her fists to pound on the locked door, to insist that her father let her go.

No, don't!

She paused. As frantic as she was, if her Papa knew that she still wanted to leave their cottage, he would never open the door.

So, with great effort to behave in a calm and resigned manner, Belle softly knocked on the door.

"Papa?" she called quietly, meekly.

"I'm here, sweetheart," he said. "I've slept outside your door, all night."

"Papa, you were right. May I have some tea? My head hurts from all the shouting last night." She hesitated. "I apologize, I didn't mean to upset you so."

An audible sigh of relief could be heard from the other side of the door.

"One moment, Belle—I'll bring your tea to you."

Belle stood, gripping the mirror in one hand, and waited by the door.

What was taking him so long? Was he on to her?

Finally, she heard her father push something heavy away from the door, and the lock clicked open.

"Be careful, sweetie, the tea is very h—"

Belle pushed past her father, knocking the tea to the ground, the delicate teacup breaking into pieces. But there was no time to turn around, no time to apologize.

She ran into his bedroom and slammed the door, locking it.

"Belle!" he yelled. "Come out here this instant, young lady!"

The only reason he wasn't as panicked as he should have been was because she hadn't gone for the front door. He didn't understand that there were other means of leaving the house. But he would soon.

The golden ring gleamed from his dresser top. Without pause, Belle slipped it onto her finger and twisted it. Once. Twice.

"I love you forever, Papa," she cried out.

Three times, and she was gone.

11

THE ENCHANTMENT

The air shimmered around Belle, the very dust particles themselves seeming to burst into flame. Oh, it was too warm, hot, like being too close to the stove—like being *in* a stove.

But then the shimmer dissipated, and the air around her cooled. The magic settled, leaving her feeling woozy and disoriented.

She looked around for a half a moment, confused—*where is my Beast?*

Her luxurious bedchamber in the castle surrounded her. The ring had taken her back to the spot from which she had left, back when the Beast was still alive, when he was still hers.

Belle set the looking glass down hurriedly and ran out of her suite, stumbling down the corridor, passing the portrait of Prince Frederick.

Run, run, find the Beast!

She nearly fell down the grand stairway in her haste, and tore through the great hall, her footsteps echoing off the stone as she ran.

"Beast!" she cried. "Fairies, open the door!"

The fairies complied immediately, the door swung open, letting in a rush of cold air as the heavy castle doors lay ajar. The air was silent, too silent. Not even the whisper of the wind in the trees could be heard. Only the rushing of blood through her ears as her pulse raced.

The Beast lay, so still, on the cold stones at her feet, just outside the door. She ran to him.

"Beast?"

Her voice sounded child-like, scared, to her ears. She *was* scared. Terrified. More terrified than she had ever been when the Beast first loomed over her in that dungeon.

"I never meant for this to happen," she said to him, but he didn't open his eyes. "I wanted to be here! I *needed to be here.* God, what have I done?"

He wasn't moving. Belle's own breath in the cold dawn air was visible, but his was not. The Beast had no more breath to give.

His fearsome face looked softer in death, as if all of the anger and animalistic tendencies he had adopted over the years had been whisked away along with his life.

"You can't leave me," she said, tears rolling down her face. "Fairies! I wish him back to life! I will never call on you again if you just bring him back, bring him back."

One tear landed on her lip, salty, and the taste took her back to a seaside trip she'd made as a child. Belle had nearly drowned back then. She licked her lips, tasted her tears. She was drowning now.

She clasped the Beast's heavy hand in her own, and collapsed on top of his bulky form.

"I should have stayed with you when I had the chance, my Beast," she said. "You are good. You are good *to me.* I don't know what happened ten years ago to change you, I don't know what your past has been like. But you are my future. Please, please come back to me."

Belle's tears fell onto his chest, and she clung to him, the same way she had clung to the stranger who rescued her from the sea, that day long ago when she thought she would fall under the water, and never come back up.

"I'm drowning, Beast... I need you."

The wind whipped her thin cotton dress around her body, freezing her to the core. She huddled closer to the Beast, as if he might warm her even now.

"I love you," she whispered.

She meant it with every fiber of her being. Closing her eyes, she pressed her ear to his chest, and quieted, wanting to hear if maybe, just maybe, his heart would beat for her, the way hers did for him.

But the Beast's heart was still.

Then—

is his heart beating?

It couldn't be. But it was! Faintly at first, then stronger.

Belle opened her eyes, but couldn't see. The wind whirled around them both, but it was if the wind had transformed into fire. Glittering magic swirled, obscuring her vision.

What is happening?

She held on tightly to her Beast, her true love. He seemed to be slipping from her grasp.

"Don't take him from me!" she cried.

No longer could she feel his fur beneath her cheek, and when she reached her hand out to touch his face—

"...Frederick?"

Frederick, half-naked, lay sprawled on the stone.

Have I fallen asleep? "Frederick, what have I done?"

He sat up, looking around them as the fire dust settled, leaving behind only a shimmer of the magic that had taken her

Beast.

"Belle," he whispered, and embraced her.

Oh God, his embrace felt so real, so strong. "Am I dreaming?" she asked.

"We're awake, Beauty," he said. "You've saved me."

"I killed the Beast," she whispered, and looked away, unable to face him, knowing that Frederick, above all, wanted her to be with the Beast. To love the Beast.

"Look at me," he said tenderly.

She gazed into his eyes, his beautiful, green

(human)

eyes.

"I don't understand…" she said. The conclusions that were forming in her mind made no sense, none at all.

"Yes, you do." Frederick smiled, and stood, pulling her up against his chest.

"I thought you were imprisoned in the castle. We've only met in my dreams," she said, shaking her head, but laughing, laughing over her tears.

"You broke the spell that changed me into a Beast all those years ago," he said. "It's still me. You know me, both prince and beast. *You know me*, Belle."

And he kissed her, wrapping his arms around her, hugging her close.

He picked her up and carried her over the threshold of the castle door.

"Fairies, we need a fire," she said as he kicked the door shut behind him with his foot.

No fire appeared.

Belle felt heat warming her face. "Oh. I told the fairies I'd never call on them again if they'd bring you back."

"The castle's enchantment is over," Frederick said, grinning. He knelt by the fireplace to get the fire going. "Although I always thought it was quite adorable how you thought we had a fairy infestation."

Belle raised her eyebrows and laughed. She had Frederick, and…he was her Beast, too, on the inside, at least. Or was it that the Beast was Frederick on the inside, this whole time? They would have many long hours in the evenings ahead to mull it over.

"Who needs fairies, anyway?" she said. She had everything she needed. Except… "My Papa will be distraught that I've left him."

"He can visit," Frederick said, finally getting the fire going. "And he can see that I am not the Beast he once feared."

"What will happen, when I fall asleep, if I don't have my dream-lover to ravish me?" Belle left the chair Frederick had set her in, to kneel by his side at the hearth.

"At night, my Beauty…you will have the Beast."

With the flames burning brightly, and the morning sun streaming through the windows of the castle, Belle felt completely surrounded by love and light.

"I love you, Frederick," she said. "All of you."

He kissed her. "I love you, Belle. You are my everything."

Though they no longer had fairies at play in their castle, Beauty and her Beast held the magic of their love close to their hearts…and they both lived happily ever after, together, forever.

~*The End*~

ABOUT THE AUTHOR

New York Times and *USA Today* Bestselling author Shoshanna Evers has written dozens of sexy stories, including The Man Who Holds the Whip (part of the bestselling MAKE ME anthology), Overheated, The Enslaved Trilogy, and The Pulse Trilogy (from Simon & Schuster Pocket Star).

Her work has been featured in Best Bondage Erotica 2012 and Best Bondage Erotica 2013, the Penguin/Berkley Heat anthology Agony/Ecstasy, and numerous erotic BDSM novellas including Chastity Belt and Punishing the Art Thief from Ellora's Cave Publishing.

Her two bestselling non-fiction writing anthologies include How To Write Hot Sex: Tips from Multi-Published Erotic Romance Authors, and Successful Self-Publishing: How We Do It (And How You Can Too).

Shoshanna is also the cofounder of SelfPubBookCovers.com, the largest selection of instantly customizable, one-of-a-kind, premade book covers in the world.

Shoshanna Evers has been listed on Amazon as one of the "Most Popular Authors in Romance," as well as on the Contemporary Romance, and Erotica "Most Popular Authors" lists.

Reviewers have called Shoshanna's writing "fast paced, intense, and sexual…every naughty fantasy come to life for the reader" with stories where "the plot is fresh and the pacing excellent, the emotions…real and poignant."

Shoshanna used to work as a syndicated advice columnist and a registered nurse, but now she's a full-time smut writer and a home-schooling mom. She lives with her family and two big dogs in Northern Idaho.

Shoshanna Evers wants you to stay in touch!

Like erotic romance?

Sign up for Shoshanna Evers's mailing list

ShoshannaEvers.com/blog *to be notified when a new book releases (right side of the page!)*

Visit **ShoshannaEvers.com** for monthly giveaways and red-hot excerpts!

Let's be BFF's!

@ShoshannaEvers Twitter.com/ShoshannaEvers

Facebook facebook.com/shoshanna.evers

Goodreads goodreads.com/shoshannaevers

****To my readers:** If you enjoyed this book, I'd love if you could leave an honest review! Reviews are so important, thank you for taking the time—I really appreciate it!

www.ingramcontent.com/pod-product-compliance
Lightning Source LLC
Chambersburg PA
CBHW021100130626
46552CB00005B/2198